THE DRAGON'S
BOOK TWO:

Dragon's Inferno

SR Langley

Published by The House of SoRoL
100 Colne St.
Castleton
Rochdale
OL11 2UG

***

***

Sign up for my Newsletter here:
https://www.srlangleywriter.com/subscribe-contact

Check out my Website here: https://www.srlangleywriter.com

(Receive further information about the worlds of Dragon's Erf... and lots, lots more!)

The Dragon

****

Vigilant guardian - reptile to ravage,
Bat-winged, war-worm, with power of thunder,
Emblem of nature - sovereign or savage,
Menace of maidens, to pillage and plunder
The kingdoms of Man, bring wisdom or waste;
Fashioned for razing the earth, dust to dust,
The foe of the knight, the foe of the chaste,
Emblem of evil, of bestial lust!
On Parthian standards my figure is flown,
Or carved in the prows of viking long-boats;
On shield of Saint George or shield of Saint Joan,
Fierce figure unfurled - on carnival floats!
Duality's dragon, blood-cold, heart-hot,
More ancient than dreams of time, long forgot!

*****

Oh world-weary worm, brave warrior's bane,
I, as the symbol of majesty's might!
Far longer than kings, far longer I reign-
For I am forever, by fate, forged to fight!
In glory of Heaven - furnace of Hell,
Before origin of sin made its snake,
As fires and lavas and fumes cast their spell
Of concocting the potion of life in a lake,
Seething contortion, some ungodly brew
of lizard-like life, of muscle and bone,
Of adamant hide and supple sinew,
As eagle clawed creature, born out of stone,
Congealing and cooling in volcanic nest
Of magna found drooling from earth's treasure chest!

Ouroborous, kin of my skin; such a snake,
Swallowing its tail in eternal torque,
That symbol of Gaea! Make no mistake
In manner and meaning, my tongue is a fork,
My breath is a fire, my scales are as ice,
Glimmering, gleaming in ophidian sheen;
For I am the keeper of virtue and vice,
For eons the creature with no in-between!
In lands of the west, I signify sin,
In the east, beneficence, worldly-wise,
Both yin and yang, as I end, I begin;
See all of time in my smouldering eyes -
For I am the dragon, silver and gold,
Like the bones of the earth - Oh God, so old!

*****

SoRoL

(From ~ Jaxx - the Mad Jester of the North's ~
Book of Serious Jokes)

Contents

PROLOGUE

Morgrim, Fire-Worm Lord of the Core and brother and advisor to the ruler of the Core, King Morgrave, was worried. His increasingly erratic twin was more than obsessed with the death and destruction of the Under Erf's True Dragon Dynasty – the Sivads.

Lord Morgrim had long planned for their overthrow and ultimate demise; in fact, for a thousand years and more now. But he had done so, step by step and piece by piece and always from the shadows. As the Core's foremost Spy Master and Counsellor to the King, he had been able to play the various factions of the Core and all Under Erf Realms and even the hated surface of the Over Erf, one against the other, fomenting disquiet and dissatisfaction and promoting his own lackeys in all three Erfly domains.

Whereas his bigger and brasher twin brother had now reached boiling point in his fanatical and mindless desire for death – especially of that nuisance of a Dragon Queen, Sivam Sivad, and her as yet unhatched third Egg, Prince Regor Sivad.

Unfortunately, King Morgrave had no care at all for the longer view and subtler arts; the more strategic and nuanced arts required to patiently play the various pieces and make the required moves, as one would as a general or a politician, upon the vast checkered battlefield-board of Planet Erf.

Morgrave was neither of these. Neither General nor Politician. All he believed in was brute force and all he cared for was immediate obedience and his own personal gratification and the Core could freeze over for all he could care, as long as he got what he wanted and when he wanted it. For King Morgrave lusted only for power and glory and that was focused most keenly on his fanatical obsession with finding and killing the last of the Sivads, the Dragon Queen, Sivam Sivad.

"Damn him to the Deserts of the Over Erf!" Lord Morgrim swore, as he left his mad brother still resolute on pursuing that nuisance of a Dragon Queen and her Egg.

"How dare he dismiss me like that, with orders to cover his fat ugly tail with the Lords of the Core Conclave, while he just goes blindly blundering about to get his prey, no matter what. I cannot tolerate this disregard and abuse any longer!"

Indeed, King Morgrave had just refused Morgrim's persuasive attempts for him to return to the Core, and not to give chase to the Dragon Queen. Despite all the other Ten members of the Core Conclave getting increasingly difficult to control and placate. The King was far too prone to taking long and unexplained absences from his Court, not to mention his tendency for brainless outbursts of anger.

"I must return to the Laboratory of Dr Rab Idego immediately, under Skiltland," he thought to himself urgently. "There I must quickly appropriate even a prototype of his infernal Mind-Cap invention. My brother must be controlled at all costs."

Morgrim well realized that if his brother went too far and lost control of that somewhat touchy and unpredictable temper of his, then all his well-laid plans could be sabotaged and a thousand years of cunning and patience would be wasted.

The secret Laboratory where Doctor Idego presided over his hand-picked team of Psychonomists and Scientists, lay deep underground beneath the Skiltish Capital of the Isle of Arid, off the west coast of Skiltland. And was yet a day's boring travel away, literally... boring, even for a powerful tunneling expert like himself.

The Fire-Worm Lords of the Core could melt and move through any rock and also control most minds, in fact their only rivals in the mental magicks and skills were the True Dragons of Under-Erf. And they also possessed incredible, magickal powers over Fire and Erfquake; but their powers waned the further they roved from the Core.

"Morgrave is a fool to venture after even a weak and wounded True Dragon so near to the surface." Morgrim mused to himself with irritation, as he burned and melted through the stratums of rock ahead of him.

Morgrim burrowed his way through the Erf's mantle rock like a fish swimming in the sea. Although he wasn't as fast as when in his normal habitat, at the Erf's Core. But there was nothing else to be done. His brother had refused to listen to reason and was even now in hot pursuit of the Dragon Queen, who still lay trapped and wounded, not far beneath the Great Forest of Lundun and dangerously close to the Erf's surface.

"It is strange though that she has somehow befriended two Humdrum children," he mused to himself as he burrowed onwards. "I cannot fathom what on Erf she hopes to gain from such a strange alliance. These Humdrums are a weak-minded, greedy and cowardly race. They are so easy to mentally manipulate and have no strength at all, let alone any magick arts. Maybe the Queen is wounded in her head as well as her body?"

Several hours later Morgrim was still ploughing onwards heading like a molten arrow of fiery hate towards the Secret Lab beneath the Skiltish Isle of Arid, when all at once a loud Pre-Call note sounded off in his brain. This was a brief but insistent rumble and blast of drumroll-sound sent from the mind of one Core Lord to another as warning of their intent and need to communicate on an urgent and immediate basis.

"Hell be in Heaven! What can that wet weasel of a worm want with me now?"

Morgrim immediately recognized this particular Call note as belonging to that of the wily Fire-Worm, Lord Morgaunt, of the Core Conclave. One of his fiercest and most cunning rivals, which he couldn't ignore. He could of course mask and control all incoming and outgoing telepathic communications, but it was very important he didn't arouse any further unwanted attention and suspicions.

He fumed to himself, but as always ensured his own thoughts were kept safely masked and concealed. He could tell that Lord Morgaunt had already travelled a long way up from the Core to within but a few hundred miles of him and he needed to ensure that he came no further. He must be kept away from his mad King of a brother!

"Hello, my dear friend, O illustrious Lord Morgaunt, how can I be of service?" Morgrim cautiously telepathed in response, in his most winning and unctuous manner.

"I wish to know, O dear foremost of Advisers to the King and Master of Spies, just where our esteemed and noble ruler, Great King Morgrave, the Wise and Wicked, may be, just at this particular moment? Can you advise us of his royal whereabouts, O most loyal, trusted adviser to our mighty King?" Came the immediate, sarcastic reply.

Morgrim had to think fast. He well knew that Morgaunt would not be seeking him out for no good reason. He would have some foul and dastardly reason of his own, simmering away and ready to spurt into action like a hot-spring geyser, at any moment. So, he would have to handle this insufferable distraction with great tact and diplomacy.

He knew that Morgaunt would quickly use any mental slip he made to his own personal advantage. He quickly prepared himself mentally for the forthcoming battle of wits and words and then answered the Worm Lords question.

"Why, how nice of you to enquire, O most mighty Morgaunt. I can assure you that the King is very well and is at this very moment setting his seal on a great victory.

He will be returning to the Core within a day or two and will then announce to you and all your venerable colleagues the details of this, his latest conquest."

"Hmmm, well, I am pleased to hear that." Morgaunt mentally purred to him. "And if you could be so kind, my Lord, just where has this mighty victory taken place; where exactly is our great King Morgrave at this very moment?"

"My apologies, O Morgaunt the magnificent," Morgrave replied, "but I am unable to tell you. The King has sworn me to secrecy on the matter. But I can assure you, he will return to the Royal Court within three days, at the most."

"Ah, harrumph. Well... I see... I see." Lord Morgaunt telepathed back rather grumpily this time, but quickly recovered his silky and soothing tone, and continued, "You see, my dear Lord Morgrim, the Conclave insists upon the King attending to his duties at Court. He has missed far too many Core Court sessions and... well, there are rumours... rumours as to his state of health and... well, to not put too fine a point on it... his mind too, you see..."

At this Morgrim judged it was the right time to go on the offensive.

"How dare you slur my brother that way! Lord Morgaunt, I am shocked at your seemingly bald and brazen utterance of such treasonous calumny!" he mentally roared.

This sudden outburst had the correct and desired effect. As Lord Morgaunt's tone immediately became more apologetic and obsequious.

"My dear Lord Morgrim, please, I assure you I am not party to such false and defamatory statements. I am a humble and loyal subject of the crown. But I have been charged... erm... excuse me, asked, to seek out you or the King himself and to ask for his attendance at the next Core Conclave. You see, my Lord, there are urgent matters that must be attended to; and not just those of the extermination of all of the Under-Erf Dragons and their unworthy royal Sivad rulers."

Morgrim smiled to himself. He had this upstart of a snake where he wanted him. "Oh, do excuse me, Lord Morgaunt, as my brother's advisor and his Spy Master, I am of course well aware of such rumours... and I am sure you yourself hold no views of any similarity whatsoever. I know just how true and loyal a subject you really are, after all, I have so many reports on your acts of loyalty and support for my brother's Kingship."

"Yes, yes, of course. Yes. Very loyal, of course," Morgaunt now burbled, being quite shaken and taken aback at what Morgrim may well have been implying by that. "But can I please have your assurance, Lord Morgrim, that you will see the King attends the next Core Court session, in three days' time. It really is very needed you know!"

"Yes of course, my dear Morgaunt. Do excuse my outburst. I look forward to attending the Court in three days' time... and with our noble King as well, of course."

Morgaunt's telepathic connection was then severed and Morgrim was left with his own glowering thoughts.

"Damn him and all his cronies to bathe forever in the blood of blasted angels!" he swore to himself heatedly. It was now more imperative than ever that he get his fat and stupid royal brother under control as soon as possible.

With that urgent need burning in his seething, black heart, he doubled his efforts to get to the hidden Laboratory under the Isle of Arid, as fast as core-wormily possible.

CHAPTER 1:
MAGMA RISING

Roger Briggs and Mary Maddam had climbed up the Dragon Queen's back and had at last entered the darkly rising slope that led to their promised freedom. Promised though only if they could make it without encountering further monsters from the Erf's Core. Such deadly things as the dreaded three-headed Trydra or mindless armies of acid-spitting Minion Worms, all of course mentally controlled by the Fire-Worm Lords of the Core themselves.

The slope's dust and smoke were still roiling all about them and so Roger had quickly equipped them both with a couple of his ever-ready handkerchiefs; these being tightly tied around their mouths and noses, making them look like a couple of misplaced cowboys.

Roger and Mary had just said their farewells to the noble but mortally wounded Dragon Queen, Sivam Sivad; or just Mavis, as she was now known to them. And tragically, this most beautiful and wondrous creature was due to explode and die sometime during the next day.

For when a Dragon gave birth to her third and her final Egg, she was irrevocably destined to self-combust within a matter of days. And Queen Sivam Sivad's time was now nigh.

But the two children were now oath-sworn to protect and carry her last Egg to the surface and to see that it arrived safely at some unknown place called the Dragon's Nest, somewhere deep in the very heart of the forbidden Forest of Lundun.

But their assigned task was far from being a simple one. Mary herself was badly hurt after her dangerous fall from under the mys-

7

terious Smoking Tree and down the long, smoky slope, to the Dragon Queen's cavern where she had been miraculously saved by Mavis.

And just as Mary had been saved by Mavis Roger now realized it was up to him to save them all, Mary, himself and the Egg, too. If that was at all possible that was.

He'd duly calculated, with his usual scientific acumen, that it was still the middle of the night up above them, reckoning it had been roughly about 2am as they'd begun their cautious ascent up the stairway Mavis had blasted for them with her hot flaming breath.

And Mavis had also given them some added protection, at least for a while anyway. Roger had no idea how long their auras of magickal blue flame would actually last though.

The Dragon Queen had opened her jaws wide and breathed out a long, billowing cloud of her magical blue flame, engulfing them both. This glowed all about them and the sloping stairway too as they climbed upwards into the ever-deepening darkness.

"*You now have the protection of the Blue Dragon Flame,*" she had telepathed to them. "*This will protect you as you climb the slope to the Skylands. But remember, trust in the power of the True Dragons - and in each other. All three of you. As you do, you will each grow and learn and will be of great comfort to the other; now, Goodbye and Fare Well.*"

And so, Mary had put the Egg safely and snugly up her jumper and tied her coat over it, with Roger's scarf this time. And they'd begun their journey to the surface and hopefully, eventually back home, back to the human world of Under Lundun and their mundane and humdrum lives there; for supposedly, up in the human world magic did not exist. Or at least that's what everyone believed; or was taught to believe.

The dreaded Governmental Psychonomy saw to that!

"Now keep right behind me, Mary, besides our auras we've only got my old torch here to light our way and I don't know how long that will last," Roger called out to her.

"Well, at least we know the only direction we've got to go is up- wards," Mary smiled, "and look, there's one of your discarded hankies, Roj, we're right where you came down."

The two weary children made their way up the murky, molten stairs, cautiously stepping forwards and upwards. The dull, red glow of the Dragon's Cavern dimming distantly behind them. Mary was still limping slightly and Roger's torch was a smudge of pale, yellow light, weakly probing the all-enveloping darkness ahead.

"*Goodbye my Children... and Fare Well*," were Mavis's final thoughts, that came softly into their minds as they made their way, step by step, up their Stairway to Heaven.

After a few minutes they had laboriously progressed some way up the makeshift stairway, but Mary was now feeling decidedly and in- creasingly queasy and out of breath too. She really hadn't wanted to say anything, but her long fall and then all of the subsequent under- ground battles had shaken her up a lot. She secretly felt that she'd probably cracked a rib or two.

Whatever her actual injuries were though the truth was that the non-stop, nagging pains from her bruised ribs and swollen ankle were slowly draining her energy, if not her resolve.

Roger noticed that Mary was slowly flagging behind him. He was growing more and more worried. Just how in the Dizzy Darwin was he going to get Mary and the Egg safely back up to the surface, let alone then to trek through the Bad Wood, and in the middle of the night too, with Mary in this condition?

But just as Mary hadn't wanted to admit to how weak and in pain she felt, Roger also didn't want to confess to how inadequate he felt for this ridiculously dangerous task; and how hopeless it all seemed too. He didn't even want to think about how they were go- ing to get the Dragon's Egg to the mysterious, hidden 'Nest' either. And the further they stepped their way onwards the more Roger's foreboding grew.

"OK if we have a quick break now?" Roger asked Mary gallantly, secretly thinking she would really need one but wouldn't want to sound weak and burdensome.

"Yes, thanks, we could both do with a bit of a rest, Roj," Mary sighed heavily in relief. "And there's nothing like having a nice little nap when yer deep under the ground with a Dragon's Egg strapped to your tummy - and a wounded Mother Dragon, not far away and about to explode anytime!" She added with a wry but strained laugh.

"Well, at least you've still got your sense of humor!" Roger laughed back. "But Mavis won't be exploding anytime soon, Mary; she said she'll guard the entrance to the slope and make sure we have plenty of time to get up to the surface and away before that happens."

And then they heard it, all about them, the sudden sound of terrible roaring and rumbling. It differed from the sounds all of the earlier Erf-quakes had made though, Roger thought, but just as to why exactly, he couldn't really say.

Roger saw several large boulders come tumbling and rolling out of the fog ahead of them, heading down the slope and right towards them both. Some way up ahead of them the slope's floor had just exploded, and pools of seething, red magma were now bubbling up and flowing downwards. The initial force of the eruption had tossed chunks of rock and debris into the air, and it was these that were now raining down upon them!

Roger realized that if he didn't move fast, they'd be crushed before their journey home had hardly started. He grabbed hold of Mary's arm and pulled her to one side, just in time, as a large boulder went crashing by, just exactly where she'd been standing.

"Quick, Mary, keep rolling; right over to the side of the slope and squeeze into any crack you can find there!" Roger cried to her, as he too threw himself onto the ground and rolled to the rocky wall at his side of the slope.

Luckily most of the boulders were careening down the middle of the slope like bowling balls bouncing down a bowling alley. A couple did hit the side walls and cracked into smaller pieces, missing them but showering them with pebbles and dust.

And some of the larger chunks went hurtling over their heads, barely inches from their scalps, as they lay huddled, face down and squeezed tightly into fissures in the rocky walls. Mary on one side of the slope and Roger on the other.

But the rock-fall was over almost as quickly as it had started. The last shower of pebbles went skittering by and just dust and darkness remained. "Whew, that was darn close!" Roger called out to her, peeling himself away from the tight crack he'd been wedged in.

But there was no answer. Mary just lay by jammed in the rock wall, silent and still.

"Are y-y-you, all right?" Roger anxiously asked, scrabbling over to her and grabbing her shoulder and giving her a quick but gentle shake.

But she just rolled over and lay there unmoving, on her back, with eyes tightly closed.

Roger's heart froze, his breath choked in his throat, and his stomach tightened to a hard, cold knot. He was absolutely terrified that Mary had been hit by a rock and had been killed.

He just couldn't bear the thought that he could be all alone now, here with his only friend, desperately needing his help, and him not being able to do a thing.

"Not a single, stupid thing to save her!" he bitterly thought to himself, as he carefully pulled her away from the crack and tried to see if there was any sign of her having been hit.

"Oh, Mary, Mary, please don't be dead," he implored, tears now streaming down his cheeks.

He couldn't see any immediate damage though, but Mary was unconscious, or... worse. She lay there, limp and unmoving in the smoky gloom. He took her and held her in his arms, cradled her head against his chest and softly told her that she was all right and that she'd soon be awake again; fumbling at her wrist to try and find a pulse.

"You're just having a r-r-rest, aren't you?" he whispered gently into her ear and smoothing her long chestnut hair with his sooty hand.

His torch had been knocked from him, but there, about a hundred yards up above, he could see the slope was still flooding with bubbling magma, now slowly seeping from the crater.

He could also see that Mavis's marvelous molten stairway ended just a few feet above them. The sloping passage above him was lit with orangey-red light, from the tentacles of magma, lazily oozing their deadly way down towards them. There seemed to be no escape. There was no going back and no way forward either. They were hopelessly trapped!

Not being able to feel a pulse, Roger bent his head over Mary's chest and listened to see if she was breathing, but he still couldn't tell.

He was beginning to panic. He actually knew all about taking pulses and getting a breath on a mirror, but that was all well and good up on the surface at some Boy Ranger's exercise for a field merit badge. But this was real life and deep underground in the dark and with red burning hot magma now looming over their heads!

Roger started to feel cold and numb. He felt paralyzed with fear and indecision. He knew he had to calm himself down and act rationally. Or they would both be dead... and very soon!

He then noticed his hand was covered with something wet and sticky. He brought it closer to his eyes and gasped. He saw that it was covered in what looked like blood. He then quickly realized Mary was bleeding. He gently lifted her head and soon found a nasty wound on the back of her head, just where a jagged rock had struck her a glancing blow.

He carefully wiped away the blood from her head and neck and then used one of his trusty hankies as a head-bandage for her wound. Then, as he sat there, unsure as to what to do next, her eyelids fluttered open and she stared up at him, groaning with a puzzled expression.

"Oh, thank all the Seven Sacred Sciences!" Roger gasped. "You're alive Mary!"

"Ooh, my head hurts! Wh-wh-what happened, Roj, what's going on?" Roger could hardly speak he was so relieved.

"You just got clipped on the head, by a r-r-rock, Mary. I really thought you were a g-g-goner there, you know; you really had me w-w-worried. You really did!" he stuttered.

Roger turned away, hurriedly wiping away his tears, putting on his best brave face for her. But now he had to tell her what they were facing up ahead of them.

"It d-d-doesn't look good, Mary," he said, trying his best to sound matter of fact about it. "We've got a river of b-b-boiling lava oozing down from further up the slope; it's just above where the steps that Mavis made finish, I think. Our Stairway to Heaven's definitely ended, and now we've got hot magma rising up instead! I don't know how we're going to get away. If we go back down, we'll just be trapped with Mavis and be blown up when she explodes."

Mary looked up the slope and saw the deadly red rivers of fiery lava, slowly sliding down the rocky slope towards them. "They're just like sticky tongues of fiery treacle," she thought.

Then, suddenly, they both heard the cool tones of Mavis speaking inside their heads again.

"Dear Skylings, I fear that this is more of Morgrave's evil doings! I must warn you that without you closer to me I am unable to protect you from Morgrave's mind-warping powers. He will do all that he can to fill your minds with fears and doubts; he will try to unhinge and confuse you. Pray, do not heed him, be true to yourselves and to your own hearts! Whatever you may see or whatever he may tell you!"

"You m-m-mean that this might not be real as well; he might just be making us see and hear all these things, and what's happening right now isn't really here? Like all this magma rising up and coming down onto us?" Roger asked Mavis, amazed and alarmed.

"No, my Sky child, what you witness now is real, but what you actually believe is well within his powers too. What Morgrave far prefers, is to enter your minds and thereby into your hearts, if you let him. Therefore, you must banish all your fear. For fear becomes terror. Terror becomes Insanity… and then you are lost and you are his forever.

"Then what the Moldy old Mangoes is really going on now, Mavis? What's just made this rockfall happen and now this lava stuff that's attacking us?" questioned Mary, with alarm.

"Mary, it's just an underground river of molten magma forced upwards from a deep Erf chamber; and it is Morgrave who is commanding its course up to you and forcing it away from its usual route, in order to attack you. For Morgrave has great magic to control fire as well as to warp minds!"

"By Kepler's Kippers! So, Giant Erf worms and Isopod balls won't do any good against that sort of thing, now will they!" exclaimed Roger fiercely. "Then, what do we do, Mavis? How do we escape?"

"I can sense the magma ascending toward you, Roger; a hot, writhing snake; but a snake of molten fire. Morgrave is even now controlling its rate of speed. Remember, he doesn't just want you dead, what he wants, mostly – is the Dragon's Egg! However, do not fear; you will have the means, you will find the way, but you must trust and Know Your Selves!"

But before they could get any specifics on what 'the Way' exactly was, or just how they were supposed to trust and 'know' themselves, their heads were filled with a thundering burst of mind-numbing noise, making them both cry out and wince with pain.

It was King Morgrave, the deadly Fire-Worm Lord, now in their heads and telepathically communicating to them from his prison-cave far away, many miles beneath Mavis's cavern.

Roger could immediately tell that this ancient and vast mind was more powerful, deadly and evil than anything he could ever have imagined!

CHAPTER 2:
MIND WARP!

Roger looked at Mary and could tell she was hearing him and experiencing the same pain too. Morgrave was cruelly taunting them, with a deep and distant voice, echoing menacingly in their heads, sowing his sly, sickly seeds of fear and doubt into their startled young minds.

"So, my poor little Egg-Slaves, has that toad-slime of a so-called Dragon been telling you her lies? Well, let me assure you both, she only wishes to have you serve her and has no real care for your lives; her lies will only bring you pain and death!"

"Don't listen to him, Mary," Roger cried. "Remember, he just wants to scare and confuse us; all he really wants is the egg!"

"Oh, Roger, what do we do?" Mary mind-cast to him; her mind, despite Mavis' warning, now in a state of barely controlled panic.

The relentless tide of fiery sludge above them was getting ever nearer. It came on very slowly, sliding down the slope, its glowing, groping tentacles hissing and spitting at them as it advanced.

"Oh, my poor, foolish, frail Humdrums," came Morgrave's deep, soft tones, "do not be ashamed at falling for that Queen Slug's clever tricks. She will tell you anything to save her own skin. You have no proof even, that the egg that you carry is hers and is not mine!"

"Oh sh-sh-shut up!" Mary cried out. "You're the one that wants to kill us! You're the one who hurt Mavis and who sent those monsters to kill us, aren't you?"

"Meee!" said Morgrave, sounding shocked and appalled at the idea. "Me! Kill You! What a shocking and appalling idea! I don't wish to harm you, child, I just wish to recover my egg that is all; I have no other wish, I assure you!"

"Wh-wh-what do you mean – your egg?" Mary asked appalled. "It's Mavis's egg and we have to look after it and see that it hatches all right, see?"

"D-d-don't listen to him, Mary! He knows you're hurt and in pain; that's why he's picking on you. He's just lying, I know he is."

Morgrave hearing this now turned his full attention to Roger.

"Oh, my wise young Humdrum; you KNOW this do you?" he said, barely concealing his bitter sarcasm. "Do you know the whole story then? Do you know how this winged-worm and all of her kind have been busily exterminating the most ancient and proud race of all the Erf? My kin, the Fire Dragons of the Core. It is she who lies! She has stolen our last egg and her mission is to see that it never hatches!"

Roger felt caught between two clashing rocks. Morgrave had a point, he had no proof at all. How did he know for certain that the egg was really Mavis's?

He hesitated in replying and Morgrave quickly turned his attention back to Mary, knowing that in her damaged condition, she was the weaker of the two.

"Come, sweet child," Morgrave coolly cooed inside Mary's head, "you need not fear me; come to me; I will prove to you that what I say is true. Look, see before you the river of magma that comes sliding downwards, to burn you up; see now, how it halts at my command!"

Mary gasped in amazement and much relief as the long tongue of deadly flames, now only about twenty yards in front of them, indeed, now came to a sudden stop. Despite all the laws of physics and gravity, it just sat frozen and immobile; steaming and bubbling, with its hot, hungry flames, flickering in the air and lighting the sloping passage they were so desperately trapped in, with a bloody red glow.

"You see my dear, my sweet Humdrum child, my darling dainty, I will not harm you at all; I use my Fire Powers purely for self-protection. I only come here for my egg. Please give it to me and I will see that you both get safely back to the surface; I promise you."

Now Queen Mavis, in her cavern not very far below, had listened to every word. And she was increasingly incensed at Morgrave's brazen attempts at undermining her as the true mother of her egg and she now telepathically interjected with a fierce exclamation of disgust.

"Ugh! You vicious, lying villain! You will not sway these human children, Morgrave; their hearts have already been tested and they have been found to be noble and true. No matter how you work and wheedle their minds with your devious words, you will not win their hearts!"

Mary stood silently on the slope; her hands crossed over the warm bulge of the dragon egg. She felt very dizzy and confused. Morgrave was still in her head and kept on at her in constant, compelling tones, telling her to come to him and he'd prove to her that what he'd said was true. He was in fact, slyly increasing her sense of confusion, exhaustion and above all, her pain.

Roger could see that Mary was in mental turmoil. She now took a couple of paces towards the frozen stream of molten lava. Roger clutched at her arm, but she just stared on ahead. Her eyes glassy and her face strained with a frown, as she bit her lip and took yet another step forwards.

"Come to me, my child, I will show you the truth; you deserve the truth, come to me and you will know the truth; come to me, come to me now. I will make all your pain go away!" Morgrave continued to gently urge.

Roger now acted and gripped her hard by the arm. "Don't listen to that lying worm, Mary!" he urgently yelled to her. "He's just m-m-messing with your mind, you know he is. Come on, Mary, don't listen to him; I know you're hurting, b-b-but, please, snap out of it!"

Morgrave then gave out a mighty and menacing, mental roar; making Roger clutch at his temples in pain. While he was distracted,

Mary broke free from his grip and took yet another step towards the river of fiery magma, although no longer moving forward, still hissing and bubbling away, with its evil heat not far above her.

"Come to me, my child, I will show you what you need to know; look, I will cool the flowing lava, so that you may cross it safely, I promise; just come to me, come to me now with the Egg - and all your worries and your pains will be ended!" Morgrave hissed sweetly in her mind.

Immediately, Mary saw that the river of magma had indeed started to congeal and harden. And Mary saw that what Morgrave had said and promised, was true. The fiery river had ceased to flow and had cooled; and maybe, just maybe, Morgrave could make her pain go away as well! She clung to that thought. Oh, if only the pain would stop, and this nightmare could be over!

Roger could tell that she wasn't thinking logically. In fact, she wasn't really thinking at all. Mary felt very tired and very sleepy. She believed that she just needed to get this all over and done with and then she could just lay down and rest, and at last be at peace.

"Yes, sweet child!" murmured Morgrave, in her mind, "you will rest, forever. I promise!"

Roger had had enough. He knew he had to do something, so he did. He stepped forward and took Mary firmly by the shoulders, shaking her and commanding her to wake up.

"Wake up, Mary! Come on, it's me, Roj, your Knight Irritant; come on now, don't give in to this wily worm! Listen to your own heart, Mary, you know what's really true!"

"Ow! What are you doing, Roger? You're hurting me, stop it, please stop it!" Mary yelled.

"Yes, my child, he is hurting you! You mustn't let him hurt you, you must stop him!"

Morgrave mentally gloated. "He isn't your friend Mary; he just wants you in more pain!"

Mary reacted and grabbed Roger by the hair and swung him around, tripping him with a fancy Judo move her Gran had once shown her. Roger tumbled down onto the rocky floor, cracking his head and rolling back down the slope for several yards. Mary, cradling the egg in her hands, moved further up the slope, drawing ever nearer to the steaming magma.

Roger, his head dizzy with pain, got to his feet and with horror, saw that Mary seemed intent on obeying Morgrave's insistent commands. He yelled out to her, mentally, as well as out loud, but she just ignored him. Mary was now very close to the edge of the magma and was about to step onto its cracked and crusty, but still red-hot surface.

"Come to me child, my fiery lava river will not harm you but will bring you safely to me! Do not fear me, my dear; come to me, come to me, come to me."

Roger could hear the echoes of Morgrave's chanting in his own mind too; the Worm Lord was incessantly beckoning Mary ever nearer. Roger instinctively knew that once Mary stepped upon Morgrave's enchanted river of fire, she would be his and the egg would be lost forever!

Morgrave's concentration was now entirely on her.

"You must find the way and bring her back to us!" Roger heard Mavis, in his head again.

With that, he leaped forward and raced back up to Mary and caught her by the arms just as she was about to step onto the steaming fiery lava field. He quickly spun her around to face him, not bothering to say anything at all. He knew this wasn't the time for trying to reason with her; this situation, just needed action.

He gave her a sharp slap around the cheek. She stood, momentarily stunned and in shock, but then a spark of slow recognition came into her eyes. He again took hold of her by her shoulders and looked at her lovingly, and called out to her, willing her to come back to him.

"It's me, Mary, Roger. I know you're hurting and you're very tired, but I won't let you go to that horrible m-m-monster. I'm s-s-sorry - but I just won't; I, I love you too much Mary!"

19

Mary looked at him and then her dazed expression changed to a puzzled one; then a slow and weary smile spread across her face. Roger could hear Morgrave in their minds, now hissing and screaming in rage and frustration; ordering them to hate each other and to tear each other to bits.

Mary came to herself though and started to laugh, although she still felt wobbly on her legs. Roger kept her upright, with an arm around her waist. Then he joined in the laughter too.

"You silly, silly old worm!" he thought with her, telepathically communicating to Morgrave. "Your senseless lies have no power over us, we are of the True Dragon kin!"

"*Yes, very good, my brave, young Egg-bearer; very good indeed!*" came Mavis, mind-casting, coolly and encouragingly to him.

Morgrave though was very, very angry, and once again was on the offensive. Any pretense at being the egg's true owner and his being a friend to the children had completely disappeared, like smoke blown away in the air. He now thundered and fumed, cursing at the children and the Dragon Queen. Luckily the terrible and atrocious swear words he was using were in the Core Worm Language, so neither Mary or Roger understood him. But they got the intent!

Morgrave resumed the attack of the fiery river of magma once more. The main thing that had stung him though, and struck at the heart of his evil power, was Roger's loud declaration of his love for Mary. This was by far, of the greatest anathema to him. Love indeed acted like a potent poison to any of his vile kind, them being the True Lords of Hate!

Roger and Mary clutched each other in a tight embrace, both expecting the worst as they felt the crackling heat climbing higher about them. The magma flow was again sizzling and burning its way forwards. The air becoming a shimmering sheet, prickling their skins as the temperature rose steadily ever higher.

They shuffled slowly backwards, trying to get away from the ever-advancing wall of flames.

"Well, what do we do now?" Mary winced at Roger. "Looks a bit hopeless really, don't it?"

Mary then gave Roger a kiss on the cheek. "I'm sorry I got you into this, Roj, but thanks for saving me; although you really shouldn't hit a lady you know." She winked and grinned at him.

"You are both truly of the Dragon Kin, children, and now is the time to use your Dragon Powers; I will help, but you must try and use your own Magical gift of the Blue Flame!"

Roger took hold of Mary's hand and they stood facing the approaching tide of fiery magma. As they stood there, unflinching in the knowledge of their loving friendship, they began to glow, in an ever-brightening blue aura. They shimmered and shivered in a bubble of blue dragon fire; they became two blue, human-shaped flames, radiating as brightly as two new-born stars!

Then they heard Mavis softly saying, *"Walk now, children; walk forward and have no fear."*

"We can do this. Mary," thought Roger, realizing Mary was struggling with the Dragon Magic. Surprisingly, Roger was finding it easier to perform than Mary was.

"Yes, I know," she murmured, weakly smiling at him and giving his hand a quick squeeze.

They went hand in hand, right up to the brim of the lava flow, and together, stepped onto it. They waited for a heart-pounding moment, but nothing bad happened. They didn't sink into it. And so, step by cautious step, they made their way together, up the long and redly simmering tongue of Morgrave's fiery lava flow.

The flames licked all about their legs and roared and flared and hissed in ever-increasing rage, as Morgrave bent his mighty mental powers towards wreaking their fiery destructions. But no matter how high or how hot the flames grew, With Mavis's mental help, Roger and Mary had discovered they could control the Dragon's magical Blue Flame, and so walked on unscathed.

Roger had rapidly mastered the magical, blue-fire abilities. But Mary had only assisted him, as best she could. She still felt weak and disoriented from the pain her body was in. A clear case of the Spirit being willing but the Flesh being weak.

Also, Dragon Magic was something that Roger definitely took to more naturally anyway. Neither knew it yet, but Mary had a very powerful magic, all of her own. But she would only discover that – if she ever did – if they made it home alive!

Morgrave's plan had been thwarted. And despite his cursing and raging, Morgrave could do nothing more to hurt them. They were impervious to his threats and his flames.

They came to the edge of the crater from where the hot lava flowed and very carefully skirted around it. Roger peered inside and saw that it went down a very long way. It was like a gaping, red-raw throat, Roger mused, ready to swallow anyone falling into its hot and hideous maw.

The flow of fiery magma had now come to a halt behind them and had cooled once more with a thick, crackling crust again forming over it, making their journey all the easier.

It seemed for the moment at least, Morgrave had withdrawn from the battle.

They stepped off the rim of the fuming crater, at its far side; Roger gallantly helping Mary down and then continued on their way, up the smokey slope, towards freedom.

"Well, Holy Boyle and Hammy Bacon! Let's hope that that's the worst of it!" Roger gasped, leaving the congealing ooze of the lethal crater smoldering behind them.

Mary just nodded her agreement. The blue aura of dragon flame now dying away from their bodies, and as it did so, the full weight of Mary's pain and weariness fell heavily on her again.

The magic of the blue flame had now dimmed back to a faint red glow. Roger's little torch had been lost so they had no other light for the last part of their journey up the inky, black slope to guide them.

After a short while, the red embers from the lava flow had died out, under a thick, gnarled crust of hardening rock and they were once again in complete darkness.

"Careful, Mary," warned Roger, "there were holes in the ground ahead of us here, made by those Erf Worms I told you about; we'll have to feel our way ahead very carefully now."

"Oh, hold on a sec, Roger!" Mary told him. "I've got something here that will help us out. Sorry, I forgot about these, till now." Then fumbling and searching in her pockets, she pulled out the sprig of moon-berries that she'd just picked earlier that day up in the Bad Wood.

The moon-berries still shone like miniature moons, much stronger than Roger's old torch and so they were able to proceed and ensure they didn't fall prey to any hidden crevices and cracks. But this turned out to be only the first of three very good and magical things that occurred.

Roger held the moon-berries up to light the way ahead of them. As he did so he gasped in astonishment. About twenty yards ahead, there were several long, writhing tentacle-like things, twisting their way down the slope and heading straight towards them.

"Oh, by Faraday's Fish-hooks! Are these friends or foes?" Roger wearily thought to himself.

But the sinewy, snake-like tentacles all turned out to be tree roots, and they were friendly!

Roger and Mary were now very close to the old Wych Elm Tree; the same 'Smoking Tree' that Mary had climbed. It was now definitely helping them, stretching down its tough, old roots.

The tentacle-like tree roots slowly slithered, snaking down towards them like several cautious elephant trunks, eagerly sniffing out currant buns. They came crawling and coiling around Roger and Mary then gently but firmly lifted them up in their sinewy coils. They were then pulled up, ascending the final hundred yards or so of the slope. The tree's long roots, being the second of the good and magical things that made quick work of the rest of their journey.

Very soon, they were once again at the bottom of the cliff-face where the crack between the smoking tree's roots had swallowed them up, first Mary and then Roger, just a few hours earlier. It was just this last cliff that they had to climb, and they'd be back on the surface at last!

But the tree roots paused in their ascent and instead of taking them straight up to the surface they uncoiled themselves and deposited Roger and Mary on the ledge at the base of the cliff.

By the moon-berries silvery light, things were clearer to see now, and there half hidden at the bottom of the cliff, Roger saw a strange, shadowy shape.

This now moved from out of the tangle of roots and rocks that made up the thirty-foot-high cliff-face, revealing itself to be a small imp-like creature, about three-foot high and a sleek, inky black all over, all except for its glowing red eyes.

And that was. the third decidedly good and magical thing that had happened.

"I amz Nimp ver Night Imp," it said. "And I amz here to take youz ter zee ver Tree-King!"

CHAPTER 3:
NIMP.

"Wh-wh-what..." Roger spluttered, taken aback, while Mary just gawped open-mouthed.

Roger and Mary had been startled half out of their wits at seeing such a very unexpected visitor. The dark-skinned Imp was fashioned like a small, skinny Demon and the strange, inky creature now moved towards them and became even more visible in the moon-berries' silvery glow.

Roger now noticed a few more details; it was hairless and smooth like a jet stone and had two small black horns on its forehead and a long, black, sinewy tail, barbed at the tip, just like an arrow. It was completely naked, and Roger could plainly see, somewhat to his embarrassment, that it was definitely male.

Mary had noticed all these things too, but despite being very tired and in pain, she was still the first to notice a detail that was the most important one of all. Nimp had a big smile on his face and his face was a kind and friendly one. She instinctively knew that, despite his seemingly negative appearance, here was a creature of good and noble values and of high moral worth.

Roger on the other hand, wasn't so sure and was therefore much more cautious. His mother had a habit of reading-out-loud the many hellfire and brimstone passages from the Holey Biblios; So, all the so-called Demons of Hell were very well known to him.

"Well, hello, Master Nimp," Mary politely replied, "just who do you want to take us to see?"

"Ver Tree King," replied the Night Imp. "I amz here ter help youz, I amz a friend."

"OK But what or who is this Tree King chap anyway?" asked Roger, somewhat brusquely. "And how do we know you're a friend, you might be working for Morgrave for all we know?"

"Oh, Roger, don't be rude! You shouldn't judge someone just by appearances you know," Mary admonished.

"Harrumph!" Roger grunted. "What else are we going to judge them by then?"

"On what they do, silly!" Mary answered simply and emphatically. Then she hobbled forward towards Nimp, and said, "How do you do? I'm very pleased to meet you I'm sure, Master Nimp. My name's Mary." And graciously offered him her hand.

"Jusht Nimp will dooz," replied Nimp, taking her hand in his and giving it a quick firm shake. He was quite used to others jumping to conclusions at his dark and demon-like appearance.

Mary noticed how warm and strong his small hand had felt in hers. She turned toward Roger and decided she'd better introduce him to the Night Imp herself.

"This is Roger, and he's a bit wary of strangers but you'll get to know him, he's a good egg really," she told Nimp. "Well, you'd best lead on then."

Roger looked on rather glumly but said nothing, just nodded and moodily thought to himself, "Well, we'll see. The Devil is as the Devil does, you know."

Nimp then gestured for them to come close to the cliff face and there the tree's great roots once more came to life and coiled around them and then gently raised them upwards.

Roger could hardly believe it. It seemed they were about to make it to the surface after all!

They were barely a few feet off the ground though, when Roger suddenly felt a strange itchy sensation in his lower legs. He tried to look down to see what was happening, but the tree root was wrapped around his waist obscuring his view. But then he looked over at Mary and saw that she too was kicking her legs about and looking very agitated and alarmed.

"There's something on my leg Roger, and it's not a tree-root!" she yelled over at him.

Then Roger saw them. Several large, fat White Ants, or more correctly, Termites, he thought. "Where the blistering Bacon and Boyle did those things come from?" he wondered.

They were busily gnawing away at Mary's ankles and Roger quickly realized, that was exactly what was happening to his own legs too.

Luckily, they were both wearing thick, woolen socks but they knew that wouldn't give them much protection for long at all.

The Termites were about three inches in length, much bigger than the normal Erf-size Termites, Roger realized. They were a pale white and rippled and oozed like fleshy maggots, but ones with sharp black mandibles and scratchy black legs with hooked feet.

"Oooowww!" Mary suddenly screamed. First blood had been drawn.

Roger soon followed suit, as he too felt the biting sting of a Termites mandibles.

"Theez are agentz ov ver Core Vormz. Morgave az zent vem!" Nimp called out to them.

Roger saw they had now drastically slowed in their ascent of the cliff-face. It wasn't only them that was under attack. The Termites were attacking the Tree Roots too!

He could see a swarm of the vile creatures running amongst the rocks and the roots and crawling out of the crumbling cliff-face in their hundreds. As he watched, shaking his legs as hard as he could to dislodge the foul beasts, he saw that the hundreds were now fast becoming the thousands. They were being deluged by a huge army of mindless, Giant Termites.

It seemed Morgrave had not given up after all!

He had instead sent more mind-controlled soldiers into battle. These ones being relatively small, unlike the Trydras, but none the less deadly, especially in such overwhelming numbers. And these Termites had but one thing in mind. To devour the Humdrum children alive and so capture the Dragon's Egg for their Master, no matter the cost.

Roger had received several bites and the tree root curled around him was now jerking and twitching very erratically. White Termites were crawling all over it and greedily eating into it, tearing chunk after chunk of woody pulp from its twisting and coiling length.

"What can we do?" Roger screamed up at Nimp.

But Nimp was busy flailing away at the deadly Termites swarming all about him as well. And being a much smaller package, he would make the Termites a tasty meal all the sooner.

But then Nimp managed to hold his black arms out before him and between his hands a fuzzy ball of darkness appeared. Growing larger by the second.

"I vill diztract themz wiv my Dark Bombz. The Tree King vill 'elp uz zoon I am zure!" he called back to Roger.

He hurled the ball of 'Dark' from him as he spoke. A great cloud of darkness hit the cliff, right where a large party of the Termites had been emerging from. The dark substance immediately choked and disoriented them, and many dropped off from the roots and the cliff onto the floor of the ledge below the cliff-face. But there were still more taking their place.

Meanwhile, the roots all around Roger and Mary were violently trembling and shaking, adding to the shower of Termites hitting the ledge below them.

But Roger could tell that there were just too many of the swarming creatures.

The Giant Termites were a Giant Hive Mind being controlled by Morgrave. And he, of course, didn't care how many of them were crushed or killed. To him they were just another form of minion low life, to be used as he saw fit in his despicable and destructive service.

But the two tree roots holding Roger and Mary were mighty limbs directly controlled by a great and powerful and sentient being; being the roots of the mysterious Smoking Tree, which was but the worldly and arboraceous form of the one and only Tree King himself!

Roger, Mary, and Nimp found themselves still coiled tightly within their tree roots, but now being brought back down to the littered floor at the base of the cliff. The roots then swiftly cleared away the debris of the dead and dying Termites and deftly deposited the three companions into a tight crevice at the bottom of the cliff wall.

"Use the blue flame Roger and protect yourself and your friends, my young Egg-bearer!" came the cool mental voice of Mavis ringing again inside Roger's head.

"OK Good idea Mavis!" Roger thought back. "I just hope I can, that's all."

"I'll help as much as I can Roj," Mary piped up, "but you seem much better at it than me for some reason."

Mary had noticed that Roger had taken to using the Dragon Magic a lot more easily than she had. She'd felt that there was something else inside her, down deep inside her very soul and her inner being, that got in the way of her taking on somebody else's magic.

Roger nodded and concentrated on producing a quivering bubble of blue flame all around them and so sealing them off from further attacks from the Termites. But it took the mindless creatures some while to realize they couldn't penetrate the bubble of blue Dragon Fire.

Within a few seconds, a semicircular wall of Termite carcasses had built up against the bubble's perimeter, where scores of the vile things had perished, just mindlessly throwing themselves against the shield and then sliding down its sides, sizzled and fried!

It was then that Roger realized that it was just him and Mary sitting there safely within the blue-flame bubble. Nimp the Night Imp was still outside!

Nimp had nimbly jumped out of the crevice before Roger had fully created his blue flame bubble and was now busily hurling more Dark Bombs and helping to clear the writhing tree roots free of termites. The Night Imp's 'Dark' exploded above him with several loud 'crrump, crrump!' noises. The tree roots would then dive into the area of inky darkness like a many-tentacled squid and swiftly sweep it free of Termite bodies.

The Night Imp and the Tree Roots are working together!" he whispered to Mary in awe.

"Yes, but there's still too many of them!" Mary whispered back, worriedly. "Look, there's even some bigger cracks appearing over there!"

And it was true. Roger looked over to where she'd pointed and saw two zig-zagging cracks splitting the cliff above them and over to their far left. From them were issuing many hundreds more of the termites. Some looked even bigger than the ones they'd already been attacked by. Roger being a budding young entomologist, suddenly realized what they were.

"Those are the Termite's Home Guard. They are the Special Forces of Termite Soldiers. A lot of these Termites are just 'Workers' and some are ordinary 'Soldiers'... b-b-but these are the Elite Troops. Look at the size of their Mandibles; they're the size of hunting knives!"

"I'd rather not!" Mary hissed in reply, hugging the Dragon's Egg tightly to her chest.

The Tree King's roots were flailing and whirling above them, and Nimp's Dark Bombs continued their explosive barrage but the whole cliff face was still swarming with Termites as they continued pouring out of the cliff-face, replacing their fallen comrades.

It looked hopeless to Roger. There was no way out. No way but down, and then only to meet another grim and explosive end when Mavis self-combusted, sometime in the coming day, just a few ghastly hours or so away.

"These things eat wood! The tree roots won't be able to keep up against so many of them, even with Nimp's help!" Mary exclaimed. "There's nothing else we can do but go back down and take our chances with Mavis!"

"No, there must be a way!" Roger replied through gritted teeth, beads of sweat pouring from him as he concentrated on keeping the blue fire bubble burning about them.

Then Nimp reappeared right before them. He was riding on one of the sinewy tree roots like a dark surfer on a wooden wave.

"Stay vere you arez children, Ver Tree King haz called vor rein-vorzementz!"

Then before either could reply, he had gone, riding the tree root as it disappeared up into the smokey gloom above them.

Roger peered above him and saw that the tree roots were all re-treating. Soon the cliff face was left totally clear of roots and only the growing army of pale, seething Termites remained.

"What's going on?" Mary exclaimed in disbelief. "The Termites will surely overrun us in seconds now. The roots and Nimp can't just leave us like this!"

"I don't know, but it looks like they can," Roger replied glumly.

But after a pregnant pause of strained stillness and silence, he and Mary soon did know. The cliff face had been a seething sea of white, maggoty bodies all crawling their way down towards them. But then the whiteness began to become peppered with black.

Roger rubbed at his eyes. He peered and squinted at the mass of looming insects and then he realized that they were no longer just Termites. Amongst all the white termite bodies were an increasing number of Black Ants.

And they weren't joining the marauding Termites, they were fighting them!

The Black Ants were still vastly outnumbered, and they were smaller than the Termites. But; and it was a big but, they were much better fighters. They were sleek and nimble and well-organized War-rior Ants. They were well organized and drilled and worked as a team.

Roger gasped in amazement as a tide of Black Ants now formed, as a curving tidal bore of destruction to all Termites that it flowed upon. A relentless wave of agile and efficient death to their slower and much clumsier enemy.

"Of course! Black Ants are the natural enemies of Termites!" Roger cried out. "That's what Nimp was telling us. That Tree King character has sent in an army of Black Ants!"

"Do you mean the Black Ants are the good guys and the White Ants are the bad ones?" Mary asked incredulously. "That's a bit 'apples for dumplings', isn't it? Usually, the white hats are the goodies and the black hats are the baddies."

"Seems like being colored one way or the other doesn't make any difference, does it?" Roger replied. "Anyway, they're not White Ants they're Termites. People call them White Ants, but they're not actually ants at all."

"Oh, alright!" Mary quickly huffed at him, stopping him from going off into one of his long scientific explanations. "The Termites have got a fight on their hands then, right?"

"Right!" Roger told her. "We'd best keep our heads down and just hope to Holy Hoyle that these Black Ants can defeat them."

Roger peered out through the flickering surface of his protective bubble of blue fire. The marauding mass of Termites was rallying against the surging wave of Black Ants. But for every dead or injured Black Ant there were at least ten Termite casualties. Roger could see that it was going to be a slow war of attrition though as there were so many of the Termites, still teeming through the cracks in the cliff face.

As Roger looked up and concentrated on the battle taking place right above their heads, he became aware of a strange hissing and chittering noise in his head. As he listened to it more intently, he realized that he was listening in to the Termite Hive-Mind, telepathically. He could hear the Hive-Mind's thoughts!

"I can hear them too!" Mary whispered to him.

"Can you understand it though?" Roger asked her.

"Yes... I think I can, Roj. I don't know how but I'm getting the drift of what it's saying. You try it. Just listen to the 'intentions' and don't worry too much about the noises."

Roger did as Mary had directed and then gawped at her in horrified amazement.

"You're right. I can understand it too. The Termite Mind is saying just one thing over and over, isn't it? It's saying, 'attack, eat, kill, attack, eat, kill, attack, eat, kill!'"

"That's right!" said Mary. "They're just horrid, they just want to eat and kill everything!"

"Can you hear the Black Ant Army as well, Mary?"

"I don't know. I haven't tried, but I'll give it a go," she told him. And duly concentrated on the wave of Black Ants still battling their way down through the main mass of Termites, that teemed across the center of the cliff face.

Roger concentrated, intently listening to them too, but it was Mary, who unsurprisingly, succeeded first.

"It's on a different and lower wavelength, Roger. But they're different from the Termites. There is a central Hive Mind there, but these Black Ants are also talking to each other as well. I think they're using their antennae to send signals to each other."

"That makes sense," Roger replied. "I bet that's what makes the Black Ants a much better organized and coordinated fighting force."

Roger could only get a fleeting glimmer of what the Black Ant Hive-Mind was saying though. It 'boomed' and 'throomed' and had something to do with, 'forward march,' and 'maintain pincer movement,' or something very like that. He didn't want to ask her, but he knew that Mary would have a more accurate understanding. She had a more natural talent for communicating with the diverse creatures of Nature than he did.

But then he 'heard' something else. It was the Termite Hive-Mind and it was changing its tactics. A large squadron of Termites was peeling away from the main mass, retreating from the ongoing slaughter, and making their way down the side of the cliff, towards them!

Soon the bubble of blue fire was being attacked yet again. But this time the squadron of

Termites had been sent with a specific and simple plan in mind. There were several hundreds of these termites in this particular squadron, and they were all being compelled to do just one thing. To prise the bubble and the children within it out of the crevice and into the open.

Roger instinctively knew that these tactics were being commanded by a much superior intelligence than the Termite Hive-Mind. This was the work of Lord Morgrave and his mind manipulation power.

The mind-controlled phalanx of Termites was now forming itself into a wedge-like shape. Maggoty body crawling over maggoty body. They weren't just throwing themselves mindlessly at the bubble this time, they were building a wedge. The dead carcasses at the pointed end of the wedge quickly became burnt and baked hard and many termites were crushed in the lower layers of the wedge. A section of the still living termites now rolled a large rock into position as the wedge continued to grow with more and more termite bodies crushed into the 'handle' part of what Roger now realized with horror, was a lever.

They were going to use the simple principle of the lever and the fulcrum and then somehow prise the blue bubble free of the crevice. The sacrifice of all those Termite minions above was just in order to give Morgrave time to get hold of what he actually wanted. The Dragon's Egg.

Hundreds of Termites now poured onto the lever's handle and the wedge of dead termite bodies bit into the side of the blue bubble as their combined weight pressed down on the handle.

Roger could see that they'd positioned the lever in the best possible place in order to succeed.

The bubble of blue flame was being slowly prised up and away from one side of the crevice. There was a definite slant in the ledge floor there that worked to the Termite's advantage.

The Black Ant Army was still making steady headway down through the main morass of the fighting Termite horde above, but Roger couldn't see how they'd possibly defeat them in time. The bubble of blue flame was rocking dangerously and would soon be free of the crevice.

The lever had grown larger and longer and Roger well knew that according to the basic laws of physics, the blue-bubble ball would soon be sent rolling across the corpse-littered ledge at the bottom of the cliff. But if he stopped creating it then they would immediately be consumed by the flesh-hungry Termites, still following their mono-manic command, 'attack, eat, kill, attack, eat, kill, attack, eat, kill!'

"Oh, Sizzling Socrates!" he exclaimed violently, "We're dead if I do and dead if I don't!"

CHAPTER 4:
THE TREE KING.

But Roger had no time to decide either way!
All at once he found himself tumbling over sideways, instinctively grabbing hold of Mary to try and save her from harm, but instead, landing on his back with her banging heavily on top of him.

The blue bubble had been sprung free of the crevice!

"Sorry, Roj!" Mary cried out, as they found themselves rolling over each other as the bubble ball rolled free of the cliff, tumbling them inside it like a couple of dice in a cup.

But Roger was too worried to reply. He could see that their protective bubble of blue Dragon fire was rolling bumpily along the cliff ledge and was heading dangerously close to the edge.

Showers of dead Termite bodies were still falling all around them from the battle above and many of these were also cascading over the side onto the dangerous slope they'd just ascended. Roger felt a surge of panic bursting in his heart and a cold, sick dread gripping his stomach.

If he didn't dispel the blue fire bubble soon, then they would be plummeted over the edge, along with the 'waterfall' of dead termites, and be sent careering down to their doom below.

At the very last moment, Roger made his decision.

"Brace yourself, Mary! Try and roll away from the edge!" he yelled to her.

With that, he mentally snapped his attention off from the blue bubble he'd been holding in place around them and they were sent sprawling through the filth and debris of the ledge floor.

Roger had calculated his timing to within a fraction of a second. Any later and they would have both found themselves hurtling through the air and crashing and bouncing back down the slope. But Roger had managed to do as he'd advised and roll with the ball's momentum, so steering himself away from the edge of the ledge.

He came to a thudding halt against the base of the cliff, his body bruised and his clothes full of bits of crushed termite. He brushed the Termite remains from his blackened face and hair and looked around for Mary. But she was nowhere to be seen.

"Where are you, Mary?" he called out. But there was no answer, just the sooty smoke swirling about him, disturbed into billowing clouds by their crashing and careening over the ledge floor.

Panic and bile rose in his throat once more. He scrambled to his feet and peered through the dirty, grey fog, squinting tear-filled eyes. But he couldn't see her anywhere.

"Where are you, Mary? Please answer me. Tell me you're OK!" he cried out again.

But still no answer.

"Oh, no! No, she can't be... she just can't be!" he whimpered to himself, choking back his salty tears. The smoke and dust were settling down now and Roger was able to see that Mary was definitely not on the ledge with him.

"Maybe I should go down a bit and see if she's just rolled part of the way down somehow," he thought. But then he stopped and exclaimed, "Oh, my Perishing Pascal! What about that hole? She could have been swallowed up by that crater where the magma came from!"

But then something fleetingly appeared through the swirling haze below him. There was something moving down there. He clung on to the stony edge with white-knuckled desperation. Then the moving shape rose before his eyes and formed into a coherent shape.

It was one of the Tree King's roots. A thick, coil of root was rising from the fog and within its coils was tightly held the limp and unconscious figure of Mary.

"Do not grieve, young Egg-bearer. Your friend and soul-mate are quite safe!" came the calm and regal tones of the Tree King himself, echoing soothingly in Roger's mind.

The tree root now uncoiled and gently spilled Mary onto the floor beside him.

He choked and rubbed the tears from his face and bent over her, stroking her matted hair out of her eyes and ensuring that she was still breathing. He groaned with relief. She was.

"Thank you!" he whispered to the mysterious Tree King.

It was then Roger noticed and realized something terrible. The Dragon's Egg was missing!

It was no longer stuffed up her jumper. Somehow it had been jolted free and been lost in all the bumping and falling. Roger knew that Mary was going to be furious with herself when she came too. But there was no sign of the Egg on the ledge either. It looked like it had gone down the slope after all. Either crushed and broken there or fallen into the magma crater.

Roger felt exhausted with despair. He cradled Mary's head in his lap, dreading the time she woke up and he'd have to tell her they'd lost their precious cargo, but at the same time wanting her to be with him awake and well again.

He was so concerned with Mary's recovery and well-being that he failed to notice another looming shape rising up from the foggy depths of the slope.

It was another of the Tree King's roots but this time it had Nimp the Night Imp riding on it just as before but now he was grinning down at Roger and was clasping tightly to his chest the Dragon's Egg. The Tree King and Nimp had again worked together, with the long, supple root shooting down the smoky slope with Nimp skillfully keeping his balance and reaching and catching the falling Egg just in time.

"You are a modern-day miracle, Nimp, whatever else you may be!" Roger exclaimed with joy as Nimp now handed him the Egg.

"Youz iz mozt velcome Mazter Roger!" Nimp replied graciously.

Then Roger realized something else!

The rain of Termite bodies falling from the battle on the cliff face above had now stopped.

He quickly looked up and saw that the Black Ants had defeated nearly all the Termites and no more were issuing from the cracks in the cliff. The battle of the Termites was over!

"The mind-controlling power of Morgrave has no more minions left here to command. We have won through and you have proven yourself a most worthy and courageous hero, Roger," the Tree King boomed proudly in his head.

But Roger really didn't feel like much of a hero. He just sighed and mentally replied with a simple, "thanks!" He didn't know what else to say. But he knew that without the help of the valiant Nimp and the quick-witted dexterity of the Tree King's roots, both he and Mary would never have made it. They would have been goners for sure.

Two more Tree roots now appeared and once again took hold of Roger and Mary and lifted them upwards in their coils. The ranks of Black Ants parted as a parade of honour to either side of the cliff-face as they passed through them, their antennae raised and quivering in salute.

Soon they were over the edge of the cliff top and were deposited, at last, onto the surface.

Roger immediately became aware of a near deafening, roaring cheer, coming from all the various creatures assembled there.

"What the Frolicking Faradays is that?" he exclaimed, as they both tumbled and rolled away from the old tree's roots and sprawled on the greensward before the Wych Elm, or the 'Smoking Tree' as they'd recently dubbed it, what seemed now such a very long time ago.

Nimp was the first to pick himself up and went over to where Mary was lying. Roger quickly joined him and returned the Egg to her. He was very pleased to see that Mary had come around, though she was holding her head and grimacing at the thudding pain she had in it, but other than that she was all in one piece with no more broken bones. She'd had a very lucky escape indeed, thanks to Nimp and the Tree King.

"I muzt apolojize vor my bad Inglishez," Nimp said to them, giving a little bow, "I amz ztill lerningz the vays ov ver Humdrumz!"

"Oh, I think you're doing very well really," Mary kindly smiled, carefully standing up and dusting herself down and wincing at the pain in her ribs as she did so.

"Hello, Roger. Well, we made it! Thanks for that. You are the bravest Knight I know!" Then turning her attention to Nimp, "Now, where's this 'ere Tree King then?" she asked.

Mary had been standing facing the trunk of the tree and so had missed and not really taken in what Roger now quickly brought to her attention. He took her by the arm and gently turned her around, so she was facing away from the tree.

"Oh, by Dickin Dookin Del!" she swore, using a gypsy phrase her old Gran had often used.

[*Dickin Dookin Del! = Gypsy slang = "Seeing with the Sight of God!"]

The great sward of green around the Smoking Tree was packed with creatures of every kind. Mary recognized the Otter family and the Goat men, the Hircumen, that they'd met earlier, but now she was suddenly confronted with creatures that just completely boggled the mind. In fact, some of them were indeed, Boggles!

She turned from one strange face to another, feeling very confused and dizzy again. In truth, she was very weak and exhausted and had been fighting on despite the constant nagging pain niggling at her all the time.

Roger saw she was in trouble though and held her upright as best he could as she went into a swoon, suddenly going limp in his arms.

"This child is hurt!" A regal voice boomed out. "Bring her a revivification potion at once."

A young goat-man came capering up with a little horn cup of 'Heartsease' and knelt at Mary's feet, as Roger held her tightly, helping her into a sitting position.

After a few milky drops had made their way down her throat, she gave a cough and a splutter and then came around again, staring up into Roger's concerned face.

"Oh, I'm so s-s-sorry about that. It's been quite a day you know; we've had all s-s-sorts..." she smiled and then came to a sudden halt, again staring in disbelief at the scene set before her.

Roger was doing the same. It really was a sight to behold.

Besides the usual Erf creatures, such as Otters, Badgers, Foxes, Horses, Deer, Dogs and Cats, etc. (the list could go on and on), there were all sorts of creatures and things that Roger and Mary hardly knew of, except in storybooks and ancient Myths, and some, not even there.

"S-s-so this is where all the animals went!" Mary gasped. "That's why the Bad Wood was so empty earlier today; they were all coming here!"

And so they were; but not just the normal, well-known animals of the wood. Mary now saw giant Spitting Spiders standing next to several ordinary Red Squirrels. And next to a small herd of Fallow Deer there were several members of the Sprite tribes: Black Satyrs, Feral Fawns and Spirited Sprites. Then she rubbed her eyes, gawping at seeing the silvery outlines of a group of tall and beautiful Elves.

Roger was likewise enthralled. His gaze took in the Flying-Rat-Bats, the Black-Bat-Cats, and many other denizens of the skies too. There were Smoky Wing-Wraiths and Albino Vampires, there were Giant Snails and Giant Erfworms and Giant Black Dogs and Big-Bog Boggarts too, all standing or sitting or crouching among the teeming crowds of ordinary everyday woodland animals and birds, now attending the Tree King's Court.

"Now, letz me introdooz youz to hiz Majesty ver Tree King!" called out Nimp, bowing and gesturing, with one arm sweeping up towards a very tall and regal-looking figure indeed, standing nearby in the shadows of the Smoking Tree itself.

The Tree King stepped before the children and Mary could see that he too had a very kindly face, but a very long, brown and wrinkled one. He stood over them, a tree-like giant of a man, twice the height of any normal sized Human. He wore a crown made of curious gem-like berries and flowers set in a thorny nest of intricately wrought branches and twigs.

He was garbed in earthy, flowing robes of green, full of leaves and berries, twigs and mosses. He was indeed a true Sovereign of the Over-wood of Inglande, the Great Forest of Lundun.

The evening scene before them was brightly lit with the shimmering lights of thousands of glowing moon-berries as he now gazed down upon the two children, first Mary and then Roger.

"A warm welcome to you both," he said. "I am, as my Night Imp has said, the Tree King. I have no other name and I need none. You children are now at my Court. It is, and it ever has been, my duty to protect all things of life within this, our Great Over-wood. But these are very grave and uncertain times and it is for this that you have been brought here - to ensure that Life and Spirit are free to go on - for many eons yet to come!"

"Oh my, sounds rather serious," Roger said, with his usual Inglishe knack for reserve and understatement.

The Tree King smiled. "Yes," he continued, "it is somewhat serious, my wee Erfling Hero, but I understand you are something of a Knight Irritant are you not – and so are well used to dealing with the 'serious' with a hearty jig and a joyous jape, is that not so, Master Roger?"

Roger just dumbly nodded. "How does he know details about us like that?" He thought, also puzzled at the Tree King's familiar manner and playfully jesting tone.

"Forgive my small jest, Roger, these are indeed serious times; but seriousness is oft best fought with some lightness and levity, is it not?"

Roger and Mary looked at each other knowingly. They had just heard the Tree King speaking in their heads, as he'd briefly done earlier when helping save them from the Termites below.

He seemed able to speak to them either telepathically, or out loud, just like Mavis had done! He now continued in telepathic mode, privately explaining some of the recent events to them.

"I have had my trusty Ambassador, Nimp here, assigned as your guide and your protector. And he well knows how off-putting his appearance and his shadowy skills are to you Humans, so he has guided and protected you the best that he could from a distance. Indeed, he would have introduced himself to you when Mary had finished climbing within my smoky old head, but for the unfortunate 'accident' of the sudden Erfquake that caused her to fall and slide her way so precipitously to the Dragon Queen's Cave. For this I humbly apologize, Mary; although it was not our intention, this was that vile creature of hate, Morgrave's doing. But now know this, children; it is all the powers of my realm, the powers of Nature herself, that I and Nimp and all creatures here, will willingly wield for you and for the Dragon Egg's protection."

The Tree King paused and looked solemnly from Roger to Mary and back again.

"But why didn't you just send Nimp after me sooner; he could have helped me get to Mavis and Mary all the quicker," Roger protested, out loud, "I was left all alone to do it all by myself?"

"Because you, my young hero, had first to discover and demonstrate your own true worth; If you do not believe in yourself, Roger, then you cannot expect others to do so!"

The Tree King's mental tone now turned softer and lower, as he continued his mind-cast.

"However, all this is but the skin of the apple. It is the True Dragons and their might and magic that truly reign within the Under Erf. My own and my subject's magical skills do not go beyond the depths of my own tree's roots. But I know well of the problem of Morgrave and his wily brother Morgrim; and of the current plight of the Great Queen Sivam. You see I am

in constant telepathic communication with her and know of what you carry, and what must now be done!" he finished, with a last and very meaningful look at Mary and her 'pregnant' bulge.

Mary stood in silence, her hands cupping the tell-tale lump of the Dragon's Egg beneath her coat and then with a sigh, she brought it forth for the Tree King and all his subjects to see.

"Thank you. It is good to have so witnessed the coming of the heir to the Dragon World. Now, pray be patient, oh, honored Egg-Bearers; I must again revert to speaking aloud and so address all that are gathered here. Your quest and the Dragon's plight are the concern of us all. But only a few of my most loyal and trusted High Courtiers will know all as I do. And they will be able to help you the most. My attendants meanwhile will attend to your wounds."

The Tree King now turned and addressed in a deep and resonant voice, all the sentient, woodland animals and the mythical creatures that Man had only known of as the 'Night Folk.'

All those creatures that over the past many thousands of years had been protected and guided by their King. He, being the Spirit of the Wood, that had long ago formed in the image of the Tree King of the Great Forest of Lundun. For the Spirit, the Wych Elm and the Human shaped Tree-King were as one. A Divine Trinity.

And now, as the embodied Tree King, he held, as-yet-unknown to Roger and Mary, his very last Royal Court, on this, his final Night of Nights upon the Planet Erf.

For the time of the Great Conflagration, of the Great Rebirth, was now upon them!

"Creatures of our Great Forest of Lundun, listen and attend to me now. These two Humans that you see before you are under the protection of the Great Erf Spirit. Gaia herself. They have a vital quest that is known to both the Mightiest and to the Vilest of Erf. I, of course, speak of The True Dragons and of The Fire Worms of the Core.

"As you are all aware, these represent the Eternal War of Good and Evil upon the Erf.

"Let it be known then that these two Humans, the Erf-boy Roger, and the Erf-girl Mary, are the Dragon Queen's assigned and oath-sworn Egg Bearers!

"And it is your duty, each and every one of you, to aid them the best that you can in their quest. We and they have a common enemy. I can say no more; but this I require you all to swear, that your help and your aid will always be theirs. Do you all so swear?"

The creatures of the night gave out a great cry of agreement. They cried, yelled, shrieked, grunted, whooped, croaked, chirped and trumpeted their allegiance and agreement, in whatever language or manner that they could best communicate with. This indeed was no mere logical response. Their roars and bleats and hoots; their howls and their screams, all came from the very deepest parts of their very wild but very un-wicked hearts.

The Tree King paused, acknowledging them with a nod of his grey, bearded head and then raised high his leaf-laden arms, embracing the sincerity and solidarity of the gathered peoples of the so-called 'Bad Wood.'

"My people, my friends! Our revels must soon end for I will be leaving you and will be making way for a new Tree King, indeed sooner than I had expected. But in time he will protect and guide you, and you, in turn, must protect him, especially in his tender years as a newly growing sapling and young tree. I trust you all - of whatever race, species or genus that you may be, to always lead or follow in the ways of the Great Erf Spirit. And always remember, the followers of Gaia have the trust and friendship of the True Dragon-Lords of the Underwood, and even now one lies close who..."

At that point, the Tree King suddenly broke off his royal address to his subjects.

As he did so, the two children also looked at each other with great alarm, for they too were receiving the urgent telepathic warning that Mavis the Dragon Queen was frantically telepathing to them all at that very moment.

Several of the Tree King's High Courtiers drew nearer to their King; they also being telepaths and therefore receiving the dire news from the Dragon Queen as well. The disastrous news that no one had expected so soon.

Morgrave had escaped!

CHAPTER 5:
THE ROYAL COURTIERS.

"*Your Majesty, Lords, and Ladies of the Great Wood, I must warn you: Morgrave has broken the magical bonds that tied him, some miles below where I am now. I hear him, and he is raging. He is mad and crazed with hate and lust for vengeance. He is making his way now to try to kill me and he even dares to breach the Erf's crust in his fury and fierce desire to destroy my Egg!*"

The voice of the Dragon Queen rang clearly in all the telepath's heads.

"*We hear you, oh Queen of Dragons; what do you require of us?*" the Tree King replied.

"*Nothing further now; but you must get your people away immediately, for there is no time to waste. I will warn you when he comes into my Cavern. But you must all know that I will now be joining my ancestors very soon; much sooner than you and I expected. I apologize again, your Majesty, that I was unable to avoid being the cause of your own demise. But I still have one final battle to fight it seems! Please do, as we have planned, assist the Egg bearers the very best you can and bring my Egg to safety. The Dragon Prince will one day be King and return the full powers and dragon magicks to our kind, and it will be he – if he lives – who will ensure the peaceful and harmonious future of all Erf-kind!*"

The Tree King's subjects silently awaited their Monarch's final words of command. All the known animals and all the 'unknown' ones; all the spitting spiders, the screeching rat-bats, the talking terror-trees, the terrible tri-toothed toad-stools, the gravy-grey-slime-slugs, the hideously hairy tree-snakes, the many-eyed moon-moths, the greater spotted snog-hogs, the toxical bog-frogs, the crepuscular dire-dogs and many others that no Human Humdrum had ever heard of! They all waited, spellbound and breathless. The noble Tree King now looked out over the sea of eagerly awaiting faces and forms and then with calm dignity and with a well-practiced restraint, he concluded his final speech and his fond farewell:

"Yes, even now one lies close, a great and mighty Queen of the True Dragons! But hark; even as I speak, she prepares herself for battle and for death, for the evil Lord of the Core, Morgrave, now dares to break the skin of our surface Erf; but the rule of the True Dragons will not allow it. Now you all must go immediately; run, crawl and slither; fly far and wide from this place and go hence unto safety; flee North across the River Tymes to the Bower of Lundun, as fast as you are able. This age is now done with - but one day you will return, refreshed with new life and with future hope; for when the smoke has at last cleared and the seed has been sown and the new Tree King grown, then you will return!"

Roger stood wide-eyed with wonder as he watched the sudden exodus occur. The multitudes of the Bad Wood's mythical creatures along with regular animals all slithered, crawled, ran, flew or hopped their way from the Green Acre, as fast as they could.

Soon only the inner the Court of the Tree King remained. The Smoking Tree still smoked lazily into the night-time sky; the same smoking Wych Elm Tree that was but the woody shell, wherein the Tree King had resided, when not abroad in his human shape.

The Tree King beckoned to his High Courtiers to gather themselves about him under the old tree's branches, as the congregation of Night Creatures disappeared northwards, into the woods.

"My Lords. Do quickly make yourselves known to the Egg-bearers standing before you; offer whatever advice or aid you can as you see fit. They will need all the help they can get, and it is important that they know and recognize each of you, as the allies you all are."

The Court Nobles, one by one, now presented themselves to Roger and Mary. As they did so, Roger noted that the Tree King quietly withdrew just a little distance away, taking Nimp with him for a private conference beside the tree's trunk.

There were ten High Courtiers that had remained behind. Three of these were Owls and now Roger and Mary gave out a quick gasp of recognition. The owls were Athene, Strix, and Tyton, the very same Prime Owls of Hooter's Hill, who had carried them to the hilltop, just hours ago!

The others though were creatures that Roger and Mary had never met before. They now came, each in turn, giving a bow of greeting and announcing their name and title, in brief introduction.

The first to introduce themselves were two Centaurs; one a glossy coal-black stallion with a head of coiling black hair and a bushy black beard. The other was a graceful and bare-breasted, creamy-white mare with long, silvery hair and a long silvery tail.

"I am Thereos!" boomed the stallion Centaur proudly to them. "I am the King and the Leader of the most noble tribe of Centaurs!"

"And I am Hippassiona!" laughed the lovely Mare. "I am the wife and leader of Thereos!"

Thereos scowled at his wife but said nothing. She stood proudly at his side and just gave him a quick and loving smile and the dark cloud soon passed from his face.

The next to introduce himself was a very tall and angular, bat-like person; "He's quite like a Vampire," Roger thought and then immediately felt a loud and painful hissing sound in his head.

"I am zee Duke Esproc Von Revadac and I am NOT zee Vampire zum zay I am, I am zee Lord of all zee Bat peoplesss!" The hissing subsided as his telepathic blast of anger faded away. He bowed to them and said, "I muzzt apoljize; you von't know my kindz very vell; I am zorry!"

Next, there came a giant, fat, green and warty frog who with a mighty leap and raucous croak, leapt from behind the awaiting Courtiers and landed with a loud thump right in front of them.

This was indeed a real giant of a Frog. He propped up his ample chest and goggle-eyed head on his two stumpy front legs and then rocked backwards onto his long and powerful back legs, folded against his warty, green flanks; his large webbed feet splayed out to either side of him.

His large, bulging and periscope-like eyes swiveled disconcertingly over towards the children. He then opened his mouth wide, made a few deep, guttural croaks and flicked out a very long, sticky red tongue towards them.

"I'm v-v-very sorry, Mister Frog, Sir," Roger said, "but I didn't quite understand that!"

"*Oh, pardon me doo, oh gallumphh, Egg Bearers doo,*" came the reply, in his head. "*I doo not gallumphh, speak your Inglishe tongues at all well at all at all, oh gallumphh, gallumphh!*"

"*That's quite all right,*" thought back Roger, "*we don't know any Frog at all at all either!*"

"*My name is Gorfgib the Goliath, gallumphh, King of the Frogs and the Ponds! I am very, gallumphh, pleased to meet you.*" And with that he flexed his mighty legs and with a snap was suddenly gone, landing some several feet away next to the Centaurs and the Man-bat person.

Now it was two Tree people's turn; one, a beautiful, Sylph-like Willow-Maiden holding a small but finely carved Lyre in her hand, and the other a handsome and spritely, sapling-strong youth; tall and tanned and dressed in green and carrying a sword. They both moved confidently and gracefully forward, and the youth bowed and the maiden curtsied.

"My name is the Lady Lucinda, sometimes known as the 'Nightingale'. I am a daughter of the Trees; a Hamadryad if you will; and I welcome you both to this realm of the Great Wood Spirit."

"And I too, Torvane, Prince of the Elven Folk, greet and welcome you gladly to our woods."

They withdrew and Roger now saw the familiar, to him, leader of the troop of Goat-men, Captain Caprinus of the Hircumen. He now trotted up to them and doffed his leather cap and gruffly greeted them in his matter-of-fact manner.

"I am no King nor Prince nor Lord. I am as I am, Caprinus, the Captain of the Hircumen and as such I fare you well and pledge my horns and hooves to your cause, as do we all I'm sure."

Caprinus withdrew to stand with the others and bringing up the rear, at last, came the three Giant Owls of Hooter's Hill, Athene, Strix, and Tyton.

"Welcome once more, young Human Erflings," said Athene, now speaking for all the High Courtiers, "we are very glad to see you safely back from your difficult journey underground."

"Thank you, Mistress Athene," Mary replied, politely. "We're very glad too!"

"Y-yes, th-thank you, we're happy we made it and got the Egg here too," Roger added.

"Now attend!" Athene commanded. "We Owls have now left Hooters Hill; most of the birds already having gone, flying North; and we, the Co-Primes, must soon follow, along with most of these nobles you see before you now. First, you must know that this part of the Bad Wood will soon be a very dangerous place for the Night Folk, in fact, for any folk. The Humdrum Humans will take every opportunity to take more of our Woods from us. But before we go, we have decided to help you with some special gifts; gifts most magical and most precious!"

With that Athene nodded to Tyton and he approached, swiveling his head towards them and blinking his large saucer-like eyes. Then, with several choking splutters and squawks, he finally coughed up a strange looking object from his beak; at first sight, it looked like a ball of mud. This 'ball' now rolled along the ground towards them and came to a halt at their feet.

"It's like a dirty tennis ball made from twigs and leaves," thought Roger.

"I know what that is!" Mary cried out excitedly. "That there's an Owl Pellet!"

"What! What's an Owl Pellet?" Roger asked, none the wiser.

"It's what Owls regurgitate from what they're unable to digest; like the fur and bones of their prey, which they usually swallow whole. The indigestible parts are regurgitated and coughed up through their beaks in the form of a ball; an owl pellet, just like that; but that's a really big one!"

"Yuk!" Roger exclaimed. "What on Erf do we want an Owl Pellet for?"

"Yes, you are right, child, but this is far more than it seems," said Athene gravely. "Each of the Ten High Nobles, as well as the Tree King himself, have given a special token of Erf Magic; you will find these Eleven tokens are each endowed with a powerful spell. But be warned, they can be used but once and should only be used in matters of life and death and the direst need!"

Roger warily picked up the Owl Pellet and saw that it was indeed composed of several small items. Bits of white bone, a blackbird feather, a shiny beetle-wing, a green oak tree leaf, an acorn, and other such things; all compacted into the messy ball of twig and dirt and pieces of moss and bark.

Each woodland item was a token of magical power that each of the Nobles of the Tree King's Court had hurriedly invoked and now offered as an aid to the Egg-bearers.

All of the eleven spells, one from each Lord or Lady, and the Tree King, had been quickly conjured and added to the Owl Pellet. Lord Tyton had then taken them all and had dutifully swallowed and then regurgitated them as the Owl Pellet they now saw lying before them.

One dirty-looking Owl Pellet but containing eleven very powerful Erf-magic spells.

Roger didn't want to seem rude in such company. And anyway, he had become much more aware of recent that there was indeed a lot more to the world than just the cold, hard facts of science and logic. There actually was something in 'magic' after all.

"Thank you very much, Lords, Ladies, most generous, I'm sure," he said, quickly putting it into a hanky in his pocket.

"But how will we know what each magical token does?" piped up Mary. "And even if we find that out, how do we make the magic work? We're not really used to magic at all you know."

"You will know when the time comes, child! Each token will tell you and help you in its own special way when its time is due." And that was as all that Athene would say on the subject.

Roger noticed that the Tree King had finished his private conversation with Nimp as they returned to the Gathered Nobles. As they did so, he thought he'd seen the Tree King quickly slip something to the Night Imp, something small and round that he'd folded into Nimp's inky palm. But he hadn't been able to make out what it was, and the King and his right-hand Imp were now back with the Courtiers and the Egg bearers, ready to finish their meeting and soon disperse.

"I wonder what that was all about?" thought Roger. "I'm still not sure about this Nimp chap; he looks so much like a little demon straight out of hell, it's quite scary!"

"Well, I think we are done here," said the Tree King. Then smiled down at Mary and said, enigmatically, "I've added a little something extra within the Owl pellet just for you, child," then continued, "My Nimp will see you safely through the 'Bad Wood' now. You must get the Dragon's Egg away to safety and hidden, where no threat can reach it. Then, in a few weeks, you must see that it gets to the proper hatching place and hatches there successfully, no matter what; such is your quest, you do understand that, don't you, my dears?"

"Yes, that's about the long and short of it," Roger answered, while Mary just nodded.

The Lords and Ladies of the Wood all withdrew now, each calling out their farewells and then making their own ways northward, either by foot or canter, or flight or hop; leaving the sward of the Green Acre, surrounding the Smoking Tree, suddenly feeling very, very empty.

Roger shuddered; there was a definite feeling of something momentous or maybe, more properly put, something absolutely catastrophic, building in the air.

"Followz me pleeze, childrenz, and do your beztss to keepz up, remembers we haz a Dragon under uz that'z about to explodez ant vun other who is hell-bentz on our destructionz!"

"OK, Master Nimp," Mary replied as cheerfully as she could, "we're with you, lead on MacNimp!"

But first, she turned towards the Tree King to say goodbye. But being unsure as to how to properly address such an important monarch, and in such fantastic circumstances, she just gave him a little curtsy and said, "Thank you, sir, for all your help; you've been very helpful and kind."

The Tree King smiled down at her and squeezed her hand in fond farewell.

Roger also said his thankyous and turning from shaking the Tree King's hand he followed Mary and Nimp across the broad moonberry-lit meadow, to the edge of the darkly, brooding trees of the encircling woods.

The Tree King waved to them as they went, wishing them the best of luck, the best of friends and the best of magic. "My dear, dear children, you will surely need all three!" he murmured to himself as they departed.

As Roger got to the edge of the wood, he turned and had his last look ever at the Smoking Tree and its noble Tree King. He saw what looked like a tired, old man, with long shaggy hair and a long straggly beard, dressed in a dull, long-sleeved robe, all tattered and torn but all in the darkened colors of the ancient Wych Elm Tree

The weary old King was lighting a long-stemmed pipe and puffing on it contentedly and then blowing smoke rings into the silvery, moon-berry-lit night sky. For a fleeting moment Roger had a brief glimpse of the ancient and venerable Tree King, at last being free; and able to just BE and lazily lean on the trunk of his trusty old tree and enjoy a relaxing and peaceful smoke.

Then, halfway across the sward and without warning, Roger's head erupted with a blasting screech of searing pain. He grabbed hold of his temples and fell to his knees in agony. Mary and Nimp did the same, although the Night Imp was affected less, being more adept at handling such powerful mind blasts. There were none though, other than the True Dragons, who had such great and superb mental powers, as the Worm Lords of the Core.

This was Morgrave's doing - he was back - and on the rampage, Roger realized.

They all heard Mavis yelling loudly in their heads, *"Morgrave is here – Morgrave is here!"* but the pain from Morgrave's own telepathic blast meant that Roger and Mary could hardly stand let alone think rationally.

Mary's face was white with fear and taut with pain as she fought to keep control of her panic. She well knew, more than anyone, just how Morgrave could slyly slide into a person's mind and wriggle and wheedle about, making them think things and do things that they normally would never dream of doing.

"Aaaargh! Roger, it hurts so much!" she screamed. But Roger was dealing with his own pain.

She kept a tight grip on the Egg though, despite the pain and despite the rising terror and the almost irresistible urge to run and to just keep on running blindly. Even to run back to the dark and foreboding crack between the Smoking Tree's roots and just throw the egg into it. To just give up and let the horrible, beastly worm have the bothersome egg. She'd never asked for it, had she? None of this was her fault, was it? It had nothing to do with her really, now did it?

Morgrave was indeed busily and eagerly, working his evil influence on poor Mary once more.

This time though she was stronger. She'd had a reviving cup of the Tree King's Heartsease healing potion and she'd had her wounds tended to as well. This time she was more able to resist.

Then the children, Nimp and the Tree King heard a final and desperate mind cast from Mavis, the dying Queen of the True Dragons.

"He is here! Beware, all of you, he is here, in my Cavern now! He approaches! Prepare Yourselves - for now, Oh, Erf Spirit willing, I will take him to Hell - and myself - to Heaven!"

CHAPTER 6:
MORGRAVE vs MAVIS!

Nimp pulled Roger to his feet and together they helped Mary up, stumbling on towards the trees.

"Vee muzt getz az far awayz as vee pozzibly canz," he called out to them.

Mary and Roger were still in a lot of pain though. Especially Mary. Morgrave was relentless in his mental attack on the Egg bearers, but it was Mary who was carrying the Egg and so getting the brunt of his ruthless mental attacks.

Roger again heard Mavis telepathing to them from her beleaguered cavern below.

"*The only thing I can do to help you now is… to MInd-meld with you once more; myself and the Tree King will do this together to give you extra protection. One of you will be with me and witness things only from my point of view, the other will share the Tree King's mind.*"

"*I'll go with you, Mavis,*" Roger quickly interjected, "*I don't want Mary anywhere near that evil Morgrave monster, even just mentally and under your protection.*"

"*Agreed!*" Mavis answered him. "*This is the only possible way we can protect you both from Morgrave's mind blasts; but beware, he is about to attack me at any moment and once I am gone our MInd-meld will end and I will no longer be able to protect you.*"

"Quickz now, wee muzt hold handz!" cried Nimp. "Wee muztn't be zeparated! I vill guardz youz while youz are under ver MInd-meld. But vee muzt getz to ver edge of ver woods at leazt.

"The black devil leading the blind boy!" Roger wryly thought to himself as he felt the pain beginning to drain from his head and his awareness once again joining with that of Mavis.

With Nimp's guidance, they just made it to the edge of the Green Acre and stumbled blindly into the cover of the woods there. The attack from Morgrave had thus far only been a mental one and the MInd-meld had at least saved them from the full effects of that.

Nimp had kept hold of Mary's and Roger's hands and Roger had taken a tight grip of Mary's.

They now lay huddled in a circle at the edge of the Green Acre as the Dragon Queen's powerful mind, fully encompassed Roger's mind and the Tree King's took hold of Mary's.

Their pain all at once vanished.

Roger again felt the strange, dizzying sensation of falling out of control, through black space, but after a second or two his vision cleared, and he was back in the Dragon's Cavern and again witnessing and experiencing everything Mavis the Dragon Queen saw and experienced.

Mavis had positioned herself right under the entrance to the slope and had her back against the cliff-face there. She stood on all fours, firmly ready for Morgrave's onslaught.

Roger gazed through the Dragon Queen's eyes and realized how very dark and eerie it was. He had really hoped that he'd never have had to see that awful place ever again.

There was still a large blanket of smokey cloud above them, glowing in red, ragged patches. Mavis also had coiling streamers of smoke billowing from her nostrils that momentarily made Roger feel cross-eyed when he looked at them. He could also feel the intense heat building up inside her fire-lungs, as well as feel the tautness of her mighty dragon muscles, as they waited, poised and ready for her, the last Dragon Queen, to spring into action.

Mavis arched her neck and swung her head slowly to the left and then to the right, scanning the cavern floor and deftly focusing in on the direction from which Morgrave would attack her. Then, all without warning, Roger, at last, saw the dreaded enemy, the mighty rock-eating Worm King that he knew was solely intent on their complete and utter destruction.

Morgrave slithered into view. Roger mentally gasped within Mavis's mind. The Fire-Worm Lord of the Core was huge. He was like nothing they had ever seen or heard of before. He now came slithering up through a large crack at one side of the cavern right towards him and Mavis.

He was like a segmented worm; but a hugely terrifying one; more like an elongated crocodile.

He was a Fire-Worm Lord, and Roger could see why. His very form seemed to be composed of semi-solid fire, of reds, oranges, and bronzes. His great armored body rippled like a cracked and seething skin full of blistering, hot ore. His long, serpentine body was easily over a hundred foot long; and more and more of it now slithered towards them over the cracked cavern floor.

This was really the first time Roger had seen a Fire-Worm Lord up close like this, in the flesh. Before, he had only witnessed the cowardly attack Morgrave had made a thousand years ago; but he had been much younger and smaller then. Also, it had been through the eyes of a terrified baby dragon and amidst the gloom and deadly confusion of the darkened Home Cavern World.

This was something very different; this was here and now; up close and personal!

"So, you protect your puny humdrum slave within your feeble mind, eh, O so-called, Queen of the True Dragons?" Morgrave malevolently mind cast to Mavis. "Well, all the better for me, for when I kill you - I will kill that meddling little Humdrum fool too!"

"*Whaat!*" Roger gasped. "*Is that true, Mavis, if he gets you, does that mean I'll die too?*"

"*Hush now, my Egg bearer,*" Mavis replied, "remember who speaks. A word of truth from such as Morgrave is as likely as a Snowstorm at the Erf's Core!"

"*Fair enough,*" Roger said, but still not fully convinced though.

"*Now you must lie within my mind as quietly as you can; I must now concentrate totally on the task at hand. But do not be afeared. I will release you to your own body before I depart mine, I promise you that, young Skyling.*"

"Halt, Core Worm! Do not come any closer!" Mavis cried out, in a clear and authoritative voice, now turning her attention to the steadily advancing Fire-Worm Lord.

Morgrave just ignored her command though and continued his relentless way towards them.

His huge, armor-plated bulk, half python, half crocodile, coming ever nearer,

"You will soon be mine, you poor, foul excuse for lizard meat!" he growled coldly at her. Not bothering to telepath either. His rumbling baritone echoing around the cavern and causing several small rockfalls that sent spurts of dust spiraling up into the thick, gloomy air.

"I warn you now, Morgrave, I am not as helpless as you may think. If you value your own skulking skin, then you should leave now and return to that vile hell hole you call home!"

Morgrave momentarily paused, then reared up, raising the front portion of his great, armored and ophidian-like body. He hissed and snorted, blowing a large blast of ruby-red flame, shooting from his steaming maw. His huge jaws were opened wide, revealing there the ranks of gleaming, shark-like teeth he had ready to slash and slay his prey with. Roger could easily see how deadly those teeth would be at taking on any creature of Erf, even a full-grown True Dragon!

"So, now you cower before me do you, O Mother of tiny tadpoles and Queen of flies? Prepare yourself to die, you one-winged, weak excuse for a flying insect!"

With that Morgrave sprung, hurling himself at her with all his might, and aiming directly for her exposed neck. He struck with such speed and ferocity it nearly ended the fight there and then. His sharp, talon-like front incisors cut a scarring swathe across Mavis's left shoulder as she just barely managed to twist away from his attack in time.

Morgrave slammed hard into the face of the cliff, such was his momentum, as Mavis whirled around, just missing being bludgeoned to death by mere inches. She was panting and grunting with pain though, and her eyes had become a fiery red, blazing with anger and indignation.

The Fire-Worm Lord juddered to a dazed halt. He took a few paces backwards, then again raised himself to face his foe, as did Mavis, and there they stayed, eyeing each other warily.

Mavis winced from a bloody wound, dripping from her torn shoulder; and Morgrave shook his head to clear the dizziness from the head-banging blow he'd received from the rocky cliff.

"You are weak, O poor Queen, and you will grow weaker. Why not submit to me now? I will make your death a quick one if you do. I will even let your puny Humdrums live too. Come now, what do you say, eh? Do the sensible thing and bow before me; NOW!"

Morgrave raised himself up even higher as he spoke; his voice becoming more compelling and commanding with every word. But Mavis was having none of it.

"Your Mind Tricks won't work on me, you miserable coward!" Mavis retorted icily.

She again filled her fire-lungs with flame, ready to blast out at Morgrave with all her might, and Morgrave seeing this, just sneered and laughed.

"You well know you cannot defeat me with fire, you poor, pitiful cripple. Listen to me; bow down before me now, and this will all be over. Accept the inevitable. You are trapped, and you will not now or ever be joining your ancestors; you are far too late for that!"

Mavis knew that Morgrave was just trying to needle and unsettle her, sowing her mind with the seeds of doubt and trying to make her lose the battle before she'd barely begun it. She also knew he was right. Fire wasn't the weapon that would defeat Morgrave; what was needed now, was cunning, foresight, tactics and intelligence; and as it so happened, Mavis had plenty of those. It was now time to give him a dose of his own mind-warping medicine.

"Does your twin brother Morgrim know you are here, Morgrave? Does he know how you are blindly rampaging about up here, far away from your realm where you should be ruling? What will the other Fire-Worm Lords say when they find out that the throne of the elected King of the Core has been abandoned? What will they do to you when they find out that you have rashly jeopardized their fiery realm... and just for your own secret and selfish ends?"

"Shhhut your slimy stink-hole, Slug Queen!" screamed Morgrave, now even more enraged.

In reply, Mavis blew a great gout of flame, but this wasn't the usual raging-red battle flame; this was a yellow-white flame, that swept ahead of her, forming into a swirling disc of pale fire. This was an impenetrable shield of fire-magic that kept any other kind of flame at bay.

"You will not be able to keep your fire shield spinning for long, will you?" Morgrave scoffed. "Come now, my pitiful Slug Queen, stop this delay, come to me bravely and bear your doom as you deserve; as a member of royalty; do not take such a coward's death!"

But delay was, in fact, all that Mavis was after. While the spinning fire shield sparkled like a giant Catherine Wheel, she hauled her back legs up onto the lip of the slope that Roger and Mary had made their escape by, but a little while before. She then backed herself into the slope a short way, nose kept downwards towards the Cavern and Morgrave, as she did so.

"Come up and get me then, Worm-fodder!" Mavis taunted. "Surely an old and wounded Dragon-Mother like me can't be too much for such a brave and bold warrior-worm like you!"

Morgrave screamed in rage and telepathed a searing mind-blast of pure hatred, scorching into Mavis's mind. Roger mentally winced, but only felt a mere shadow of the blast's actual ferocity. He was still being protected by the power of the Dragon Queen's mind. But the Fire-Worm Lord reared up once more, lunging at the fire shield and blasting it with his own ferocious fire-bomb. The blast exploded in the middle of the fire-wheel, causing it to weaken and slow its rotation.

Morgrave gave one more mighty blast and this time the wheel wavered and started to slowly unravel in its final wobbling revolutions.

Mavis was prepared though. She exhaled a long breath of cool, magical blue flame that soon completely covered her crouching form. She lay pressed to the floor of the slope, just waiting for Morgrave's hate-fueled charge. She knew that her taunting tactics had done the trick. She could see Morgrim fuming with blind and unthinking hatred for her and for all Dragon-kind.

That was exactly what she wanted. She wanted to lure him as near to the surface as possible, where he was the weakest. And that was exactly what she was doing.

Morgrave blindly and unthinkingly came bursting through the shreds of Mavis's Fire-shield and thrust himself forwards and upwards, squeezing his bulk on to the slope. He hadn't seen the Dragon Queen's maneuver though and didn't expect Mavis to be facing him. He roared in surprise when he saw her a little way up, just sitting there, facing him and waiting for him.

"Your magical dragon flames won't save you either, you miserable mother of slug-slime!" he screamed at her, as he slithered and crawled ever nearer.

But Mavis didn't move. Morgrim came charging onwards, smashing the slope-roof and many of the stalactites that studded the roof there. His short but powerful legs crashing into the floor and ripping great chunks out of it with his adamantine talons as he went clawing upwards.

Such ordinary rock to Morgrave was really like nothing more than soft butter to a steel knife. His glinting talons and saw-like teeth were ready to rip and rend live dragon flesh, and there was no rock on Erf that was going to get in his way.

As he came upon Mavis, he shot out from his snout a sizzling gout of purple and violet flame. This flame, a powerful type of Core-fire, was totally deadly to any and all life that it touched.

The vile, violet flame now encased Mavis in its horrible, bubbling mass of toxic fire-plasma, eating away at her own magical cocoon of protective blue-flame she had covered herself with.

"There is nothing you can do to stop me, you, useless fool, can't you see that? It is over; you are defeated - and now you will die!" Morgrave screamed at her.

Roger quailed fearfully within Mavis's mind, watching in horror as the Fire-Worm Lord loomed ever nearer as the haze of Mavis's protective blue fire was slowly eaten away.

"Oh, by the Sins of Suffering Socrates," he thought, "this looks like curtains for us all!"

"Hush now Roger, have faith!" Mavis's urgent thought coolly admonished him.

Morgrave's evil and gloating face was now but a mere few yards away from Mavis. The Fire Worm pulled all the coils of his long lizardish bulk up into the sloping passage. Mavis retreated, slow step by slow step, moving up the slope backwards and keeping her muzzle pointing straight towards Morgrave's advancing bulk.

His knife-filled jaws were again wide open, ready to slash and slay the injured Dragon Queen. The last flickers of Mavis's magical blue flame now trembled and died away, leaving the dragon (and the terrified passenger within her mind), seemingly, totally defenseless.

"At last my time has come!" cried Morgrave, in insane glee, his great crocodile-like head knifing through the air and slicing into Mavis's neck with great force. This time though, his aim was true and anyway, Mavis didn't even try to dodge him.

The hate-frenzied core worm pulled all his slithering length up and over the Dragon Queen's body. Coil after coil, tightly gripped and squeezed around her flanks, while his venomous fangs pumped deadly poison into her neck.

Then, loud and proud and clear and dear, ringing coolly in his head, Roger heard the last Queen of the Dragons calling out to him and Mary:

"*Goodbye my Egg-bearers; and Love each other, whatever else you do, Love Each Other.*"

Then the ground rocked and reeled beneath them and Roger's world became one huge and deafening drum of thunder and a cataclysmic eruption of searing dragon fire, as Mavis exploded!

Mavis had planned well. The sloping passage acted just like a gun barrel. As she exploded, she directed the main force of her energies down and straight into Morgrave's body. He screamed and writhed in agony as he was shot down the slope like a cork out of a bottle. He landed heavily in a crumpled and steaming mass of charred skin on the cavern floor below.

His body was now a mass of bloody, raw flesh. And, as he soon discovered, with a howl of disbelieving anguish and horror, although he hadn't been killed, he was now totally blind!

Meanwhile, as Morgrave went down, Mavis went up; like a rocket!

Her sudden explosive blast, obeying Newton's Third Law of Motion, "For every action, there is an equal and opposite reaction," as Roger would have gladly pointed out if he'd still been there to comment. But now, he no longer was. True to her word, Mavis had released him from her MInd-meld, just before she'd exploded.

As he came around Roger mentally saw that the Tree King and the old Wych Elm tree were once again united and now burned brightly in his final act of consummation. But Roger knew, with uncanny certainty, that his story would somehow continue. For in time, there would be a new Tree King once more, standing tall and strong in his place; ready and able to protect the woods and the magical world of the Overwood.

Mary had mentally seen and heard everything but had been kept safely within the Tree King's mind throughout. But then the violent explosion from Mavis had ripped through his roots and embroiled his ancient tree in its hot, fiery inferno, even as he released her back to her own body. As she left him though, she briefly saw and felt the hot, billowing fireball devouring his nearby human form, and soon he was gone, as nothing but dust and smoke amongst the roaring flames.

While the battle between Mavis and Morgrave had raged on below them, Roger and Mary's bodies had collapsed by the edge of the greensward and had both been lying motionless on the ground there, as if they had been in deep comas.

Nimp had stood over them as their faithful guardian though. And was much relieved when they groaned and started to come around.

"Velcome back!" He grinned at them both.

Roger just nodded, he could still hear the explosion and feel the ground quaking beneath him. He got to his knees and immediately checked on Mary. But she pulled herself upright too and then together, in total horrified silence they watched as the flames erupted all around them.

The Wych Elm tree was now definitely smoking no more. Instead, it was engulfed in a bright tower of violent, violet flame, and had quickly transformed into a solitary torch, burning and blazing ferociously in the center of the greensward, like a flaming beacon in the night.

For a short while it burned alone, hissing and crackling in the red, orange and violet flames that engulfed it. But as it burned ever brighter and hotter, streams of white-hot sparks blew from its branches, swept away by the wind into the night, and into the waiting woods surrounding it.

The world about them was steadily being turned into a whirling, mad-maelstrom of smoke and flame and scorching heat.

Soon the whole of the Bad Wood would be ablaze!

CHAPTER 7:
ABANDONED!

Great geysers of flame and smoke were exploding into the air all around them as they ran. Roger watched in awe as the conflagration took hold. Bright, sizzling, hot sparks were flying everywhere, setting more and more of the trees around them on fire. Soon there'd be a fully-fledged forest fire raging and as they didn't know which way to go; they would all be trapped!

Roger realized that he really did have to trust the Night Imp now! He could feel the fierce heat blasting and basting his sooty tear-stained face, battering him relentlessly, as it radiated from the flaming torch-like tree. He could feel his skin crawling and crinkling in its heat, as his eyebrows, cheeks, and lips became increasingly sore. He saw that Mary was suffering the same effects too. Though she was doing her best to disguise her pain and discomfort.

"Don't worry, we'll make it, Mary, we'll just have to follow this Nimp fellow and hope he knows which way to go!"

"I know, I'll try and keep up, Roj. But it's so bright up here too!" she replied with a grimace.

Both being so recently used to the dark, now had eyes that were constantly weeping, being dazzled by the brightness of the flames; especially at the white pillar of flame erupting at the center of the blazing arena, where the Tree King had once held his Royal Court.

"Are we going to die?" Mary asked him quietly, tightly gripping hold of his hand as they moved onwards through the trees, their heads kept low and their arms and hands raised in front of their faces to ward off the searing heat as well as the painful glare of the flames.

Roger just stared ahead, tightlipped, peering through his fingers, and said nothing further; there was really nothing sensible that he could say. They had both come so far and had seen so much. Surely, they weren't just going to perish here, burnt to a crisp in a blazing forest fire, unknown and all alone?

He had a dismal vision of his parents having to come and identify his smoking remains; just a pile of grey ash poured out onto a hospital table. He imagined his stern father stiffly saying, "Yes, that's him, that's our Roger. We always knew he'd never amount to very much!"

Then all of a sudden, another tremendous explosion erupted from the burning Wych Elm tree.

With a great, thunderous crack, the white, flaming tree-trunk split into two, as another gigantic gout of flame erupted from beneath it. This time though, a massive sheet of red and gold flame came gushing upwards, that quickly took the shape of a beautiful scarlet and gold Dragon. Rising high above the canopy of the burning wood. This fiery, flickering Wraith-Dragon now billowed upwards, coiling and leaping high above them, then slowly dispersed and faded away, disappearing into the vastness of the red-embered night.

Both Roger and Mary immediately knew that the very essence, the 'soul' of Mavis, had at last gone on to join her ancestors in the beautiful and joyous Dance of the Dragon Souls; high above, in the Skylands of the Spirit-world! She was now at last back home, with her much missed and much-loved Mother, Queen Anivad Sivad!

They looked at each other knowingly, both smiling, their eyes shining brightly, and both somehow innately understanding and feeling the same great rush of anticipation and happiness; the unlimited and inexpressible joy, that they knew Mavis was feeling at that very moment!

"Oh, Roger," whispered Mary, "she's all right you know, she really is all right!"

"Yes, she is," murmured Roger, softly, "you know, I believe she really is!"

And now, although they were no longer bound together by Mavis's telepathic connection, they both knew they had to move, and move very fast. It looked hopeless, but they weren't going to stay there and just get burnt to pot-ash without a struggle. They'd make a fight of it, somehow, some way. Just as Mavis had told them; in fact, as she'd taught them:

"There is always a way to find a path that is worth the taking."

The flames though were acting like they were some sort of napalm or Greckian Fire as used by the ancient Greckians thousands of years ago. They weren't ordinary flames at all. Whatever they touched immediately burst into flames and wouldn't go out. This, after all, was a fire that had been started by the self-combustion of a True Dragon.

This was a very rare event indeed, but all Roger knew was that the flames were leaping from tree to tree faster than they could outrun them. And besides, Mary was still not fully recovered from her ordeal of falling down the under-erf slope into the Dragon's cavern, despite all the help and magical ministrations given by the Tree King's attendants.

Roger reluctantly realized only the magical power of Mavis's Blue Fire could protect them from the fire's ferocious onslaught, at least for a while anyway. And it was up to him to create the blue flame required. And he wasn't at all sure that he could anymore, not without Mavis's help and guidance. And she was definitely no longer there to guide and assist him.

"Oh, blistering Bohrs and dynamite Davy!" he exclaimed out loud, feeling frustrated and fully realizing that the life-saving Mindmeld with Mavis was well and truly over, now that she had self-combusted and was no longer able to share her telepathic Dragon abilities with them.

Also, he didn't want to put any more strain on Mary's shoulders. He knew that she seemed far less comfortable and confident conjuring up the magical dragon fire, whereas, for some reason, he found it came to him more readily. Which he thought was strange really, as he would have reckoned on Mary being the one more naturally adept at such things as magic.

He knew the truth was that it was once again up to him to 'Find the Way!'

He took hold of Mary's hand, and slowly willed the magical blue glow about them once more. He felt a small thrill of satisfaction, mixed with surprise, at finding he could still actually do it.

The sparkling blue bubble of fire wobbled and wavered about the two of them, but it was enough and held its form and immediately the relentless heat diminished.

But now they had to move and move quickly, just to escape the fast-spreading fire that was burning and blazing, from tree to tree.

"Cumz on, youz Humanz, quick nowz, wee muzt go or wee all burnz up!" Nimp called out.

"OK, Master Nimp. But I don't know how long I can keep this blue Dragon fire bubble going so I hope you know how to get us out of here!" Roger replied.

For a while, Roger had forgotten all about the Night Imp. He was just a bit ahead of them and outside the fire bubble. But he now called to them urgently, in his strange, soft and smoky voice.

"Thiz vay my friendz, thiz vay, I knowz ver vayz fer uz to go, pleez, vee muzt hurryz now!"

The children could see the flickering, dark form of the Night Imp, only barely half their size, urgently beckoning to them and pointing the way to go. They couldn't make out his appearance very clearly at all though, as, amongst all the raging fire and billowing smoke surrounding them, he seemed to be made out of smoke and shadows himself.

"Come on, Mary, we've got to keep moving, I won't be able to keep this magical blue flame protecting us forever you know!" Roger called out, pulling her along by the hand. But after only a few faltering steps she came to a halt once again.

"Sorry, Roj, it's just my leg, I don't think I can run very far with it at all."

"Well, we're not staying around here and I'm not leaving you!" he told her emphatically, putting his arm around her waist. "OK, Mary, you put your arm around my shoulders, and we'll make it out together, even if we have to do it hobbling along like we're in a three-legged race!"

Mary grimaced and wiped at her sweat-streaked and burning cheeks and did as she was told. Meanwhile, Nimp was getting more and more agitated.

"Hurryz up, vill yooz? Wee muzt getz to ver Hooter'z Hill at leazt, to ezcape ver firez!"

Roger scowled but taking as much of Mary's weight as possible, continued in the Imp's wake.

"We just have to trust him, I s'pose," Roger thought to himself, "we don't know which way to go ourselves, what with all this fire and smoke; and we're not just going to give up, are we?"

So, he obediently followed Nimp and holding Mary tight and keeping her upright, helped her limp painfully onwards through the burning wood.

Mary gave him a quick look of affection. "Lead on courageous knight, lead on," she urged.

The wood all around them was well alight now; they had to dodge and dart through the falling debris of burning branches and twigs that were bouncing off the blue dragon flame shield; as well as avoid the stinging sparks and clouds of pungent smoke, that if they breathed would most surely scorch their lungs red and raw

Nimp was nimbly dodging his way through the falling debris and didn't seem at all bothered by the flying sparks and the scorching heat though.

"If we're heading for Hooter's Hill, like you say," Roger called out to him, "then aren't we likely to come across those carnivorous trees; those Whining Willows, as Mary calls them?"

"Yez, but ver Villows vill not be vanting to feed wiv ver voodz on fire, vill vay?" Nimp answered him. "Ant vee are on ver Tree King'z biznezz, ant zo vay vill not getz in our vay!"

"Well, by Einstein's Eyebrows, I jolly well hope so!" Roger muttered.

Then, just as Roger had predicted, the expected grove of Whining Willows hove into view. The flames hadn't quite reached them yet, but the Willows were all very well aware of the forest fire bearing down upon them. Even as he watched, Roger saw the first flickering tongues of flame reaching into the Willow grove's outer-most branches.

The Whining Willows weren't taking the encroaching flames lying down though.

Immediately their whip-like branches began to flail about, lashing out at the flames and trying to put them out. But they soon found that no matter how hard they beat the flames back, they still came on, relentlessly lapping at their branches and setting them alight. The more the Whining Willows flailed at the flames the more ferocious they became.

Then Mary tugged at Roger's arm and pointed into the grove of agitated trees.

"Look!" she cried. "In the middle of them, some poor creatures have been trapped!"

Roger dutifully looked and immediately saw what Mary was pointing at. He shivered in horror remembering how he had nearly been devoured alive by one of those same carnivorous trees.

There dangling from the innermost and largest Willow tree was a group of large furry animals. They were hanging upside down, coiled tightly within the supple branches of the tree.

Roger couldn't tell if they were alive or not at first but then he saw one of the largest of them wriggle a clawed forearm and then it's head free of the tree's coils. It desperately scrabbled at the tight branch trying to loosen its bonds further but to no avail. The tree sent another whip-like branch coiling around the helpless creature and soon it was once more subdued.

But Roger had seen enough. "I know what they are!" he gasped. "They're the Giant Otter family we saw back at the River Quaggy. They've only gone and got themselves caught!"

"Oh, Roger, no! But I think you're right. We have to help them!" Mary cried in alarm.

"Yes, but how? We're barely able to help ourselves right now and I don't think I can keep this blue flame going much longer either!" he glumly replied.

"Maybe Nimp can do something," Mary said, "you remember how he had some sort of influence with the Whining Willow that got you, Roger?"

Nimp had rejoined the two children, initially intending to urge them to follow him in skirting around the Willow Grove but he too had seen the plight of the poor Otter family.

"Oh, please Mister Nimp," Mary begged him, "I know we're running out of time, but we have to try, don't we? We can't just leave them to be eaten up. Is there anything you can do?"

Nimp looked at the hanging Otters and then behind him at the approaching wall of flame. He quickly calculated and realized that he only had bare minutes before the flames caught them. The outermost ring of the Willow trees was beginning to blaze, to the left and the right of them. He realized that his idea of running around the willow copse was now already doomed.

"Followz me, pleez, ant keep vat blue bubble goingz az long az you canz, Mazter Roger."

Nimp darted into the Willows and charged up to the central tree where the Otter family hung suspended amongst its drooping branches. Roger and Mary followed on behind as best they could, Mary still hobbling and increasingly in pain.

"Veez zilly Otterz vill get uz all killed!" Nimp muttered angrily. "Ztay here ant vait for me – bit if ver fire breakz through then runz for it!" He told them and scrambled up the Willow tree's trunk and disappeared into its frond laden canopy.

There was a moment's pregnant pause as the Willow seemed to suddenly freeze. It then shook its large shaggy head as in objection to something and became still again. Then another silent moment passed, and the Willow tree shook again but this time in order to untwist its long branches and free the Otters from its shaggy coils.

Whatever Nimp had said or done it had worked. The Otters all dropped to the ground and gathered together as a nervous and bewildered group close to where Roger and Mary stood.

Nimp dropped from the branches above the gasping and confused family group; Lutie the Mother Otter held her cubs in a tight embrace. Her husband, Artie now stepped forward and said,

"Thank you very kindly, Master Nimp. We are sorry to have caused you so much trouble, but the young 'uns got a bit too excited and ran off straight into these 'ere Willow trees."

"Yes, we are all forever in your debt, Master Nimp," his wife, Lutie piped up, having somewhat calmed her brood of crying cubs. "If there's ever anything we can do for you we will, but we'd best be heading off north again really quick now. That fire is getting right close!"

Nimp nodded his agreement and with that, the Otter family scampered past Roger and Mary, Artie and Lutie giving them a nod of acknowledgment as they went. Soon they had all vanished into the trees, heading North.

Roger had kept the blue flame flickering its protective aura about them but was now getting increasingly worried as to how long he could keep doing so. The sparkling bubble of blue flame was already quivering and quaking as if it might collapse at any moment.

"Vere iz only vun vay to go ant vat is through the copze of willowz. The flamez are beginningz to surround them all. Vee must run az quick az pozzible!" Nimp told them.

"OK, Mister Nimp, we're in your hands now, lead onwards, and by Albert Einstein's 'Airy Eyebrows, get us out of this awful inferno, OK?" Roger gasped breathlessly, feeling like he was acting a part in an action movie he'd seen; some exciting adventure, that when the film finished, he'd just be able to get up and walk away from and then go home – but this wasn't a movie at all, this was for real!

They followed Nimp on through the grove of Willow trees and so left the carnivorous trees, abandoned to their grisly fate of being burnt to ash in the forest fire behind them.

But Mary was wincing and hobbling badly now, and Roger had to go at her slower pace and let her put more weight onto him. They followed the Night Imp the best they could and Nimp kept a short distance ahead of them, turning occasionally to ensure they didn't lose sight of him. But flames were catching in the branches of more and more trees around them now; they just didn't seem to be able to outrun the fire at all.

Nimp moved ahead as quickly as he could with the children struggling to keep up with him, again passing under flaming trees as they stumbled desperately onward, the Night Imp crouching and hopping about like an agitated, shadow, dodging and ducking between the burning trees.

"At the end of this particular three-legged race," Roger thought grimly, "we wouldn't just get a school prize if we won, we'd get our lives!"

Then all of a sudden, a burning branch came crashing down very near to him; Roger stumbled in alarm, almost dropping Mary, but he quickly regained his balance and pressed on regardless.

"We're heading South again, back toward Hooter's Hill. If we can make it up to the hilltop, where there aren't any trees, then maybe we'll be all right," Roger shouted to Mary.

"Whatever you say," Mary winced, doing her best to keep up with him.

What Roger really thought though, but had no intention of sharing with Mary was, "I don't see us making it to Hooter's Hill at this rate at all; but I mustn't think that. We have to try, we just have to; by Socrates Smelly Socks, I just wish I had wings!"

The forest fire was a raging wildfire now, rapidly spreading from tree to tree. Wherever they trod, and in whatever direction they went, flames came writhing and reaching out towards them.

The Bad Wood was rapidly becoming a stampede of flames snapping at their heels just like a pack of wild, red Wolves, hot on the hunt for their kill!

Roger knew that they couldn't go on very much further. He could see that Mary was in pain and just about spent. But at last, they came to a rocky outcrop, a jumble of large and flat-topped rocks and here Nimp cried out for them to follow him up onto the largest rock's flat surface.

Roger pulled Mary desperately into the shade of the rocks and then hauled her up onto the pan-like surface above. She lay there, panting, with great sobbing gasps, her face a taut mask of soot and tears. And Roger wasn't in much better condition himself.

The magical pale blue aura of the Dragon Flame, that had surrounded them and had given them much needed protection, was now definitely flickering and slowly fading away.

"This really does look like the end," Roger grimly muttered, blinking his scorched eyelids and peering out through blackened fingers at the approaching onslaught of red and ravenous flames. "Where in all of Holy Hoyle's Hell do we go from here?"

He stood up on the rock, next to Mary's prone figure and searched for any sign of the much sought after, Hooter's Hill, or anything at all that could possibly save them. Before him he could see nothing but trees that weren't yet burnt and behind him the terrible scene of smoke and flame as the fire raged towards them; he could clearly see that the forest fire was spreading very fast; indeed, much faster than they could ever possibly hope to outrun, especially in their conditions!

The little Night Imp stood crouched nearby, silently surveying the scene under a raised hand, hooding his glowing coal-like eyes, peering ahead into the as yet untouched woods. He seemed to be muttering to himself and debating as to what the best course of action could be.

"This is one problem that my Science isn't going to solve," Roger thought bitterly, "this is definitely a problem that really does need a bit of Mother Nature's Magic, as Mary would say." He then turned toward the Night Imp, to ask him whether he had any ideas as to what they could possibly do. But... unbelievable horror of horrors! He wasn't there! The Night Imp was gone!

Roger and Mary were now completely alone on the lonely island of rock and were being slowly and surely surrounded by a marauding wall of all-consuming flame!

They had been abandoned!

CHAPTER 8:
OF LIGHT AND DARK
(AND IN BETWEEN)

Roger, very wearily, sat back down and took Mary in his arms and just quietly held her there, her head gently pillowed in his neck. Both their legs drawn up close as they sat, curled and huddled together as a small and lonely ball of humanity; Mary semi-conscious and completely exhausted and Roger just awaiting his hot and horrible and inevitable end.

As Roger sat, silently with Mary and the Dragon's Egg, he wondered what made a creature like the Night Imp so callous and uncaring as to betray helpless strangers as he'd done with them? He'd come along to help them he'd said, and for a short while had done just that. Then, he had suddenly and without any explanation whatever, up and left them, abandoned to their fiery fate.

It was totally beyond Roger as to why any reasoning, rational creature would behave in such a way. Is this what was meant by the old adage of Nature being 'red in tooth and claw' he mused. Was Life just a matter of kill or be killed; eat or be eaten! One for one and none for all!

The heat was definitely getting to him now. The pale blue aura of the Dragon Flame had all but gone. Once again, he protected his and Mary's face with yet another couple of his trusty, 'Cowboy Hankies, that he pulled from his pocket and tied tightly over their mouths and noses. The large rock they were on was being steadily surrounded by flames, licking hungrily through the underbrush and spreading from bush to bush and tree to tree. Very soon they would both be afloat on a lonely stone boat going nowhere and drowning amidst a sea of roaring fire!

There seemed to be no escape whatsoever. Roger to his own be-musement realized that he now actually felt quite calm and philo-sophical about it all. He was quietly amazed at himself that he wasn't running around in circles in a mad panic, screaming "I don't want to die, I don't want to die!" Of course, he didn't want to die; instead, he just quietly thought to himself how Mary only had 'him' to rely on and how he'd better show some of those 'hidden depths' she'd spoken of.

"Well, I've got Mary here and she's hurt and I need to look after her, no matter how horrible things are; it's my duty as her Knight Ir-ritant after all, and that's all there is to it!" he thought.

Mary was by now though, semi-delirious. The continual pain and difficulty in breathing had been taking an increasing toll on her ever since Mavis had exploded. She was also feeling dry and hot and so very, very drowsy. All she really knew was that she was with her friend Roger, and he was her brave Knight and doing his best to look after her. She knew that he would always do that. Always be there for her, as her courageous one and only Knight Irritant.

"My Knight irritant, night, night; Knight, kite, irritant; irrident, immitent; that's what he is, he's my night, night, imminent!" she mur-mured, babbling in her confused delirium. She lay limp and semi-conscious in his arms, with her eyes closed, and began feverishly yelling, "Must save Mavis's egg, must save Mavis's egg, must, must, must save..."

Roger whispered to her, "It'll be all right, Mary, we'll save it, don't worry, we'll save it."

Of course, he had no idea as to how they were going to do such a thing. They couldn't even save themselves, let alone a Dragon's Egg. The fire was now raging all around them and smoke was billowing and blowing in their faces too, making them hack and cough and their eyes smart.

Roger closed his eyes and let his thoughts wander and float off where they would; doing his very best to have nothing to do with the horror and the heat of the 'outside world.' The World that was now slowly but surely cooking them on that rocky frying pan; sizzling their bacons in the raging and out of control forest fire. His clothes were now beginning to curl and char at the edges and his skin glistened and crinkled in the scalding heat.

He'd always been able to just 'switch off' from the boring work-a-day world and go into his own inner world. He'd had quite a lot of practice, of course, doing this, living with the mum and dad he had. The 'Art' of being indifferent, it might be called. At this, Roger was a True Artist. As he lay there, doing his best to hold and comfort Mary and not think of the horrible death that awaited them, he suddenly remembered that there was something important that he really should remember. But the heat was making him too drowsy. He just couldn't think for the life of him what it could possibly be; not for the life of him.

"Hold on just a Max Planck Minute!" he thought. "Life! Yes, it's something to do with Life!"

He screwed up his face and pressed his fists against his temples and tried to ignore the heat and the smoke and just concentrate on what he knew was so vital that he remember. Then, all at once he got it. Fragments of what he'd been told by Tyton, the Owl Co-Prime, now came to him.

"Tokens of Erf Magic; powerful spells; Life and Death! Yes, that was it! The Owl Pellet and the magic tokens; surely there must be something there!" he thought excitedly to himself.

He rummaged in his pocket and pulled out the owl pellet. It lay there in the palm of his hand. "Now what?" he thought. "What on Edison's Erf am I supposed to do now?"

He poked at the pellet with a finger and tried to discern its contents. What was it Tyton had said to Mary's question about how to make the magic work? "Each token will tell you in its own special way," he'd said. "Well, this ball of old rubbish isn't telling me a pesky thing!" he thought grimly, scowling down at the now crumbling pile of so-called magical tokens.

As Roger sat on the rock prodding at the Owl Pellet, he realized that he was becoming more and more negative and pessimistic and was thinking just like his old self, in fact, just as he was before he'd met Mary and had begun this incredible adventure. But now he suddenly thought, "OK, so what would Mary do then? I know she wouldn't be such a sour-puss and be so skeptical about magic tokens and such, that's for sure!" He then decided he'd at least take a closer look; suspend disbelief and just, well... Look!

He took out yet another hanky and laid it neatly on his lap and started to pull the Owl pellet apart and so reveal its contents. This didn't take very long at all as it was already falling apart in his hand. After a few short minutes, he was left staring down at eleven, assorted natural objects.

And still not one of them had said a thing to him!

"Now what we need more than anything is wings or the power of flight or even a magical rainstorm; any of those will do, but what have I got? Nothing! Just a handful of old forest litter!" He muttered to himself disdainfully.

Mary was moaning beside him and he could see that the flames had now surrounded the high, flat rock they were sat upon and everywhere he looked, there were more flames and more smoke. He quickly picked up each token in turn and silently pleaded to it to just do something magical to rescue them. He paused a short while after each burst of prayer, but no answer or magic came.

The supposed magical tokens consisted of a white bone, a black feather, a twig of red berries, a small piece of brown fur, a round, shiny black pebble; a piece of green, velvety moss, a little, pointed tooth, a small, green acorn, a flat, pouch-like seed-case, a tiny mouse's claw and a shiny bird's beak. And all wrapped up in dirty bits of grass and shavings of tree bark,

"Nothing!" he thought in disgust, "just nothing!"

He wrapped up the so-called 'magical' items in his hanky but as he did so, he noticed that one of them had started to faintly glow. He peered closer and poked at the contents again, and then, yes, there it was once more a faint, yellowish glow; and it was coming from the green acorn!

"Hold ol' Heraclitus's Horses right there!" he yelled. "There is something going on, after all!"

Yes, it was definite, the little acorn was glowing brighter now, and he noticed that the more he concentrated and looked at it, the more he believed it, and the more it seemed to glow, turning into an ever brighter, miniature golden sun in his palm.

He quickly tied up the rest of the tokens in his hanky and stuffed them back into his pocket. He lifted the golden acorn up level to his eyes and gazed at it even more intently, giving it all the concentration that he possibly could and wishing fervently it would do something to save them. "Even if you can just save Mary, that would be enough!" he prayed, eyes now screwed up tight from the scintillating light of the acorn.

The more he prayed the more radiant it became, and it also seemed to be growing in his palm. It had become a bright shining, golden ball now; lighting up his face in its pure and radiant glow.

Then, clear as a bell, he heard the Tree King's wise and venerable voice, echoing in his head.

"This is my personal magical token to you, Egg bearer; the Golden Acorn of the World of the Erf Spirit! This is not the world of petty, jealous ghosts or angry, foolish gods that your human fairytales tell of, this is the world of Love and Life; Courage and Compassion; Truth and Honor! These are the greatest of all magicks there are and by your knowing more of this world and these things, you will have the greatest gift of all - Universal Understanding!"

"What on Erf is 'Universal Understanding' going to do about us being burned to a crisp in this forest fire though?" Roger gasped disbelievingly to himself, totally incredulous at his being offered something so useless and unhelpful, let alone so untimely.

As he thought this though, he quickly noticed that the acorn's bright glow dulled a little.

"Maybe I'd better watch what I think around these magic token things," he wisely thought, "seems what I think about them has some sort of effect on them, and maybe that's true for our being trapped in this forest-fire as well! Maybe there's more to this 'Universal Understanding' business than I at first thought!"

With that, he now noted that the golden acorn was once again glowing brightly in his palm.

"Right! That's enough scientific proof for me; now what do I do next?" he exclaimed loudly.

Then, with a flash of sudden insight, he knew exactly what to do.

He took hold of Mary's hand and pressed the acorn tightly between their palms. He held her hand close to his rapidly beating heart and felt its rich warmth pouring into him. The golden glow seemed to spread through his veins. He could sense the same was happening to Mary too.

"OK, Mary," he whispered to her semi-comatose form, "work with me here; let's both concentrate together; let's wish for the help we need; whether it's wings or for rainfall; or... or something else... some other sort of 'understanding,' just as long as it's something that gets us both out of here, eh?"

Hand in hand they lay there, eyes closed in each other's arms.

Then it happened.

Roger suddenly felt himself rising up and leaving his body!

And Mary was doing the same. They weren't growing wings or both riding on a magic carpet; they were though, getting away'- sort of - by leaving their bodies behind them!

Roger felt himself being caught up in a mutually shared 'dreamscape.' A shared experience with Mary and the Egg of the Dragon Prince! Mary was no longer comatose or delirious and under her coat, she still held the now 'phantom' egg wherein the baby dragon was slowly forming. Roger realized that all three, Roger, Mary and the Egg, were now fully free, but as Spirits.

However, the Dragon Prince babe would never be born, as he'd been destined to be, not if his material egg was burned and destroyed along with their own bodies on the rock below them.

Roger felt himself rising and pulling further and further away from his small, Erf-bound body. He had no thoughts or concerns about dying or about anything like that at all. This parting from his human body was a very good feeling in fact; this was something far, far more fundamental. They were now like ghosts, aware and sentient, but existing outside their human bodies!

What was happening was more than just plain, old-fashioned dying; but they simply had no real language or way to explain or describe it; either to themselves or to each other. It was only something that you could only consider real and true if you actually experienced it yourself.

Roger was floating and flying upwards, disembodied and climbing rapidly through wisps of cloud until the night sky all around him was just a huge dome of star-studded navy-blue. He went ever higher, hand in hand with Mary, with her holding the phantom Egg under her phantom coat. Their arms stretched out wide and their spirit forms flickering like two, pale candle flames.

After a short while, they came upon a huge, towering column of frothy, white cloud that was slowly rotating, like a giant wheel. Roger felt himself being pulled towards this and being drawn into the clutches of its vast whirling coil of cloud. His vision now became more blurred, both with the speed and the swirling of the cloud itself, he couldn't really tell which, but he didn't really care. He found the ride breath-taking, despite as a ghost, his not having any breath anyway!

Roger felt totally elated as he and Mary now raced around and around in long, winding arcs, high up above the Erf. They were both joyfully swooping in and out of the giant, spinning cloud, like two flying-fish, flashing in and out of an ocean's waves.

"Look, Roger, I think we've got company!" Mary gasped, pointing ahead of her.

Roger saw what looked like a large shoal of silvery fish from that distance. They were moving as one body and speeding across the rotating inner surface of the whirling, white hurricane cloud, but as they came closer, Roger could see that they were, in fact, hundreds of ghost-like figures, just like he and Mary were. But these were a whole company of ghosts, and all were enjoying themselves, having the very same ride that Roger and Mary were experiencing.

Then all at once, the great crowd of ghosts was upon them. They swooped on by without a pause and just neatly split apart and whirled on by Roger and Mary's amazed ghostly forms.

And they didn't stop, they moved as one, just like a murmuration of swifts would, or an actual shoal of silver herring in the Atlantis Ocean. But they weren't fish or birds, they were all people Roger now saw, but they were all dead, being a host of ghosts of all ages and nationalities.

Soon they had all gone and the spiraling wheel of the hurricane was Roger and Mary's alone.

At last, climbing ever higher, they flew, soaring out from the top of the cloud. There, receding far below them spun the whirling, white disc of the hurricane, that they had been gleefully riding, just as if it had been their own personal funfair carousel.

Roger hung there, high in the wide, dark attic of the sky, looking silently down upon the great spiral of cloud, as well as on the vast curve of the Planet Erf; both slowly revolving below him.

He could see the line of the dawn moving across the face of the Erf, as the sun steadily rose in its morning splendor. He could see the dark side, the side of the Night, was being beaten back, as the bright and glorious light of the rising sun poured across the spinning rim of the Erf.

Then they suddenly found themselves being pulled upwards once again, rapidly going higher and faster, up to the very limits of the Erf's atmosphere; with the vast starry background of outer space stretched out behind them. Then, hand in hand, they speedily orbited around the Erf, until they were viewing it from the exact opposite of where they had just observed the apparent dawn.

This time they could see the line of the deepening dusk moving across the planet Erf's face, far below. It was now the dark mantle of the night that seemed to steadily and inexorably march its way onwards across the planet's surface. Night was relentlessly eating away at the dwindling day and all its life-giving light. It was now the Day, that was slowly being vanquished by the steady onslaught of the advancing tide of Night's darkness!

Roger and Mary hadn't uttered a word or even made a sound. Mary though now turned her pale, glowing face towards her friend Roger and smiled.

"I can see through you; you look just like a ghost!" she laughed at him. Then she squeezed his hand affectionately and whispered softly in his head, "We're both being taught a lesson now, aren't we, Roger? A good lesson though I think, don't you?"

"Yes, I think we are." Roger quietly answered.

Once again, they floated there for a short while and just watched the rippling line of darkness spreading like an ink stain across the bright blue and green cloth of the Erf below them.

"I think it's all to do with the light and the dark somehow," Roger mused.

"Yes," said Mary, "it's all a matter of your point of view really, isn't it? That's how it seems to me anyway, we're being shown something quite important I think, don't you, Roj?"

"Oh yes, definitely," Roger quietly replied.

"Like, from one particular viewpoint, the dark's always winning, but from another, it's the light that is," Mary quietly said.

"But it isn't a matter of winning or losing at all, is it?" said Roger, "I mean, the Light and the Dark, well, they're just in a sort of continual balancing act, aren't they? Like in a game of tag, or like a crazy dog chasing his own tail!"

"Yes, one does seem to go with the other," Mary replied. "I wonder though, is dark just an absence of light or is light an absence of dark?"

"Well Mary, I don't think it really matters that much, when you're up here like this, does it?" said Roger, feeling strangely elated. "I mean it's just all a very big, old game really, isn't it?"

"Well, I'm for the Light!" Mary said.

"All right," Roger replied laughing, "then I'll be for the Dark!"

"Though mind you," Mary beamed, "I bet there's lots of fun to be had IN BETWEEN!"

The two ghost children laughed together, floating high in the Erf's stratosphere, feeling at once both awestruck and humbled. They floated serenely together, ghostly hand in ghostly hand, but fully aware they were not of fleshly form anymore. They were though, at peace and were just as they wished themselves to be; two new, young friends from Inglande. Who, right there and then, just happened to be floating as free spirits, many miles above their beautiful Planet Erf!

CHAPTER 9:
GAIA.

"What about our bodies though, Roj? Do you think they'll just be burnt up in the forest fire; that would be just awful, wouldn't it? We'd never get the Egg hatched then, would we? Our quest would be over before it even began."

"Well, we'd just have to get some new bodies somehow, I s'pose," Roger replied worriedly.

"Yes, you would – and that, of course, is your free choice, oh, children of my beautiful Erf!" spoke a cool and melodious voice in their heads. This wasn't the Co-Prime Owls, or even the spirit of Mavis, or the Tree King; this was the Great Erf Spirit herself!

"Yes children, I am the Spirit of planet Erf and I welcome you here as my personal guests."

Roger frantically looked all around, trying to locate who it was that was speaking to them. Mary did the same, but they both just remained spinning around at the edge of space, hopelessly looking for the invisible 'Being,' the Spirit of Erf who'd just spoken to them and seeing nothing.

"You children and your precious Egg have been sent here by my good friend, the Tree King of the Great Forest of Lundun, he who has but recently passed once more into the Spirit Plain. You will not 'see' me, as I am of Erf itself and indeed, I am not of one creature or of one form. But you may hear me and so may understand me. I am known by many names. Some call me Mother Nature, some Terra Mater, others, Isis or Danu or Gaia; there are many, many names. You though may choose whichever name you wish."

"*Um, we're very pleased to meet you,*" Mary said, being the first to find her mental voice.

"*Yes, er, likewise, ma'am,*" Roger mumbled telepathically and somewhat hesitantly.

"*Excuse me, your er, Majesty or Highness or, er...*" Roger's question faded away to nothing before he could even finish thinking it. He was very unsure as to how one should address an Erf Spirit or... an Erf Goddess; whatever she in fact actually was.

"*You wish to know child, am I a god or goddess? And you wish to know what you are doing here? And you wish to know whether you are now dead and whether your human bodies have been left to burn to ash along with the 'Bad Wood', as you Under Lunduners have called it?*"

Now Mary's love of Nature came to the fore. This was like a dream come true for her. Mother Nature, the one and only actual Spirit of the Erf itself, was talking to her! Her face shimmered and shone, glowing with a soft, golden smile as she addressed the Goddess.

"*Can I call you Gaia, your Majesty, if you don't mind? I've always thought of you as Gaia.*"

"*Of course, you can my dear; Gaia it is, and please, no more of your Majesty this or your Majesty that. You Mary and you Roger will know and name me only as Gaia from now on.*"

"*Th-th-thank you your M-m-ma... oops ... sorry, Gaia!*" Roger replied sheepishly.

"*Are you really some sort of a God then?*" Mary asked, "*or should I say, Goddess. You can't have a male being the Mother of Nature, now can you?*"

"*These things are but mere labels, child,*" Gaia answered. "*And all labels can easily be lies. I have no gender as you know of it. But I prefer the personification of 'Mother.' For I am the Great Spirit that the Tree King spoke of; I am the Spirit who chose to create the living Erf as you know it and love it! It is my responsibility; every mountain, ocean, river, animal, tree, leaf and tiny microbe of it! The Erf is my home and my body.*"

"*So, you are a sort of Goddess then anyway,*" thought Mary, with a defiant pout.

Gaia just laughed, filling their heads with a rippling music of laughter that made them both grin from ear to ear, lightening their hearts and making them feel that the whole universe was just one very big and very funny joke.

"Now, the answer to your second question is..."

"B-b-but we didn't ask you any questions!" protested Roger.

"But you have both thought them haven't you, dears? You wish to know why I have brought you here and what the Tree King's Golden Acorn does for you and what use is this for you? The answers are: Firstly, you are here to learn - so your questions will be answered. Secondly, The Tree King's acorn gift is to teach you that you are not your bodies! You are much, much more than that!" Gaia simply stated.

"And the answer to your third question is: Therefore, knowing that you are Spirits, your having or not having a body should be of no real consequence to you. You are YOU, however, you choose to address yourselves, or indeed 'dress' yourselves. This alone is vital knowledge, both for your own development and for the success of your quest! And now my dear children, you must choose, do you wish to stay as you are, or to return to your quest and your bodies in the burning wood below, just as you left them and as they are now? Decide - and it will be so!"

Roger and Mary floated silently enthralled at the very edge of space; silently hanging there, suspended as spirits between Heaven and Erf. The wise words of the Great Erf Spirit, of Mother Nature herself, echoing in their amazed minds. Could they really abandon their bodies like that and just exist forever as roaming spirits?

"Wh-wh-what do you mean?" Roger stuttered in disbelief. "If we stay like we are now won't we be ghosts, just like all those we saw swooping about in the Hurricane below?"

"Yes," Mary quickly added, "if we stay here as we are, then we'll both be dead, won't we? After all, that's what not having a body means, doesn't it?"

Gaia's voice chuckled kindly in their heads, "Oh, no, my dear children, the complete opposite is in fact true. Being fixed in one body is really a sort of life-terms imprisonment. You will both feel much better being free of bodies. But... you are also free to choose. You may return to my Erf and take up new human forms again if you wish, but as new-born babes of course."

"Erm, yuk... I don't fancy being a baby again!" Roger muttered, shaking his head at the thought of going through all that horrible messy business of dirty nappy changes, being winded and wiped and potty trained and such.

"You misunderstand me, Roger," Gaia answered. "You are both free to go where you will... and to take up new lives in new forms of whatever kind you wish... or... as some have already done... you may remain a Spirits, or Ghosts if you will. The choice is freely yours!"

"Do you mean we could be re-born as anything we wanted; like as a wild horse even, or an elephant or lion?" Mary gasped excitedly. "Oh, I'd love to be a wild horse, galloping without a care across the open plain on my un-shod hooves with my unruly mane blowing in the wind!"

"You have the whole of Nature to choose from!" Gaia murmured quietly.

"Well, I'd want to be at the top of the food chain!" Roger told her. "Maybe a Lion. But it would be interesting being an insect too, wouldn't it? Just imagine if I could be any insect I wanted to be, I'd really be a great Entomologist then, wouldn't I?"

"Only after you'd become a human again, Roj!" Mary pointed out.

"Yes, I suppose so," Roger agreed, somewhat deflated at the idea. "But all this supposes we always remember who we are and retain our Spiritual identities. That doesn't happen normally does it, I mean. Most people think when your dead, that's it, everything's wiped away and gone."

"There is no need for you to fear, child. You are now both fully aware of your true natures as Spiritual Beings, are you not?

They both avidly nodded their agreement.

"Then that awareness is yours now... and forever," Gaia answered. "Do not listen to those who would try and persuade you otherwise. They are but lost and fearful souls mired in the mud and mysteries of flesh and blood!"

But then Mary had a sudden realization.

"But what about Mavis's egg? What about our promise to her and our oath to the Tree King?" she anxiously thought to the Goddess and to

Roger. *"All those creatures who are relying on us to save the last Dragon's egg. We can't just abandon our quest, can we? We have to return to our bodies no matter what, we can't just give up on it all now!"*

Roger gulped... and reluctantly agreed; as soon as Mary had mentioned Mavis and the Egg, he too realized they really didn't have any other choice at all. Even if it meant them returning to their certain deaths in the forest fire below. He'd never be able to live with himself knowing that he'd turned his back on his new friends, despite having given his word to save the Dragon's Egg.

And he also instinctively knew that if they did stay, then his friendship with Mary would just eventually fade away and be over. They would not long remain friends, both well-knowing what the other had done. Abandoning their lives on Erf and their oath-bound Quest and their Honor.

They would, in fact, be no better than Nimp, the Night Imp had been.

Roger recalled with a sour taste and a bitter feeling in his heart how the Night Imp had just callously abandoned them to their fates of being burnt alive. He shivered and silently cursed the little black devil as a totally bad lot.

Then Gaia spoke again, and it was as if she had read every thought within their young minds; (which she of course had).

"Do not be so quick to judge your fellows, children! You must both learn much more of the High Magic; the true magic of Love and Trust and Truth and Hope; such as these will be the most important Spells that will pave your way to your true spiritual freedom, as well as for you fully discovering and mastering your own natural powers."

Roger immediately felt the sting of Gaia's rebuke pierce his heart; and felt ashamed.

"Yes, you're right," he whispered, *"just because Nimp betrayed us, it doesn't mean we have to do the same, does it? We don't really know what was going on with him anyway, do we? And, well, I know I didn't like the look of him from the start and I was even happy to be proved right."*

Roger felt rather guilty now as to how he had behaved towards the Night Imp. Maybe the poor thing had run out of courage and just couldn't take any more. Maybe he was just feeling angry at him because he secretly wished he could have done the same and saved his own skin!

"*You are free, children, to go where you will, as you are now. Or you may return to Erf in whatever form you prefer or to remain as Ghosts playing with the others of your kind on Erf. Or, you are free to roam the spirit plains to seek new physical worlds. The universe is full of such suns and planets and moons and many other wonders... you are free to start afresh on any you choose; grow any new body you wish. You can become a mighty speckled spider-beast of Supa-Spica 4; or even a pink cloud of pulsating, space-spores in the Arcturan quadrant; or maybe join the House of the Tenticular King Fish on Primordia; or you may yet just seek for another Human colony on any far or nearby planet. The choice is freely yours.*"

But Roger and Mary had already made up their minds.

"*We will return to the Erf, Gaia!*" Roger firmly replied for them both; and for Regor too.

"*But what if we go back to our bodies and we just die, what do we do then, Roj?*" Mary asked. "*It didn't look too good for us down there, did it?*"

"*Then we'll just come back up here and start on a new game, I s'pose; but we have to go back, we just can't abandon Regor and our promise to Mavis, now can we?*" Roger just mentally shrugged. He'd made up his mind and new there was no turning back.

"*Yes, I know you're right, but, hey, Roj! I thought I was being the Light and you the Dark!*" she answered, pouting ruefully at him.

"*Oh yeah, sorry! I forgot that.*" He smiled at her. "*Well, we can each be a bit of both, OK?*"

"*Is there anything you can do to help us, Gaia, you being the Erf Spirit and all, couldn't you just blow all the flames away with a big wind or something; can't you directly help us like that?*"

Mary asked, now fervently praying that Mother Nature would say, 'of course my child, whatever you wish for will be yours;' just like a magic Genie in a bottle would; but of course, she didn't.

"*You already know the answer to that, child, don't you? I may advise and may even teach, but my lessons can be hard to learn, but they must be learnt by the individual spirit, alone.*"

"*Yes, OK, I think I understand,*" Mary meekly nodded.

"*Good, although I will not interfere in your decisions and choices, but you must be aware, there is always a right and proper path to follow but it is you alone who must find and walk it! I will tell you this though, you have been chosen; the Erf is in great peril and must now be healed. The natural basic goodness and constructive creativity of Humans must unite with the ancient wisdom of the True Dragons... and so bring about a new era of True Civilization for all!*"

Mary turned to Roger. "*Well, I'm ready I think, Roj; let's do it, eh?*"

Roger nodded his agreement and with that, very slowly and very fearfully at first, they began their fall to the Erf. Hand in hand, descending toward the swirling spiral of cloud below them.

"*Goodbye, Egg-bearers; remember your lesson and keep to your true path!*" Gaia cried out, as they left her presence and their long fall towards the distant Erf gathered ever greater speed.

But as their fall speeded up, they found themselves once again sucked into the great gaping mouth of the spiraling hurricane cloud, they'd played in before. Roger felt the immense force of it tugging at him, but not just in the usual physical sense. He also realized as a Spirit he could be wherever he wanted to be. And this was a feeling... of raw, elemental power... of Spirit power.

But now his 'phantom-self' was being drawn ever deeper down within the spinning vortex. They both soon plummeted into the very heart and soul of the wind-howling hurricane.

Roger then realized that the Hurricane was a Being as well; a sentient spirit itself! And they were being pulled into its eye; the very place where the eye truly was the window to the soul!

"*Welcome back, Egg-bearers!*" The voice of the hurricane itself seemed to boom inside their heads, as they fell in an ever-speeding spiral around and down its heaving mass of cloud.

All around them the great walls of cloud spun dizzily by, sizzling and crackling with primeval electrical energies. They hung there, momentarily suspended within the inner central calm of the raging storm. It seemed like the hurricane was telling them that no way could they pass through; no way could they take on such a madly ferocious and unforgiving force and overcome it... for they were just children, after all, weren't they; just weak, human Erflings; so, who were they to defy such elemental forces? How could frail flesh overcome such primal power?

"Because we're Spirits and not just flesh!" Roger cried out to himself with valiant defiance. *"By Occam's Ruddy Razor! – nothing's going to stop us now!"* he yelled as he fell.

With Mary's ghostly hand still firmly in his, he focused his attention on the night covered Erf below, where he knew the Bad Wood burned and where huddled together on a hot, sizzling rock, their two mortal bodies lay, with the Dragon Queen's last Egg. But no way were they going to let Morgrave get hold of that Egg and win. They would hold true to their oaths and find a way!

"We were sent to rescue that bloomin' Egg, so that's just what we're gonna bloomin' well do, come Holy Hoyle or Herschel's Hell-Fire!" Roger thought defiantly.

They now found themselves swept into the walls of the cyclone and spun around and around, whirling faster and faster and dropping lower and lower. Roger realized that at the dizzying rate of speed they were going they were very likely to just crash into the solid Erf below and become two very shattered ghosts, left to search for their splattered and scattered pieces of Soul forever.

"But can ghosts shatter though?" he wondered. *"What if we just kept on falling – forever!"*

The world became a white blur; a wild, whirring, whizzing merry-go-round of force and fury, of whipping wind and crashing thunder. Great jagged bolts of white lightning came ripping and forking through the boiling clouds all about them. Huge sheets of electricity sizzled and seared the very air itself. They could feel the very elements themselves, roaring and raging about them as gigantic torrents of seething, primordial energy.

Roger felt they were being toyed with by a voracious vortex of primeval power; some ancient and angry God. But he was determined. They had decided. They would return to their bodies and yes, to their deaths if needs be. Roger knew with an unwavering certainty that would have totally horrified his conservative parents, that he was in fact much, much more than just a mere body!

Then with a strange and sudden 'popping' sensation, they suddenly found themselves once again outside and below the vast swirling cloud.

"Goodbye, little ones!" Roger heard the hurricane, echoing faintly in his head, as he and Mary plummeted on Erf-wards. "You may think I'm all powerful now, but in a few days, I will be dead and I will be gone... forever!"

Roger and Mary's ghostly forms spun awhile like two dice nonchalantly tossed to the fates. But as they controlled their spin, Roger could see the whole of Inglande spread out below him. And as they fell ever lower, he saw the Great Forest of Lundun, looming ever nearer and larger, coming up at them at an alarming rate.

"There it is!" cried out Mary. "There's the Bad Wood burning below us now!"

"Yes, I see it too," Roger replied, "can you see our bodies yet?"

Both Roger and Mary peered intently down into the burning blaze, that but such a short while ago had been the flourishing and florally abundant, 'Bad Wood.'

"There we are!" yelled Mary, exploding in his head with unbridled excitement. "I can see us, Roj, we're still alive I think!" Then she paused and wryly commented, "Oh, isn't it so strange, talking about ourselves like this? I don't think I've got used to it yet, have you?"

"No, not yet," Roger replied. "But I s'pose it's best we just look at our bodies as things that we have and that we use, not as things that we are."

"*Yes, I think you're right, but do you think I'll still be unconscious? I mean, when we're back in our bodies, Roger; do you think I'll remember where we've been and, well... everything?*"

"*We'll just have to see, Mary,*" he answered softly; and with that, they were suddenly back.

The rock where their bodies lay came rushing toward them and everything went totally black.

At first, there was no sound and no feeling. But then Roger opened his eyes and the horror of what lay before him became fully apparent. Mary, as he'd secretly expected, did indeed lie next to him, unconscious once again; and all around them raged a solid wall of crackling fire.

They were now totally enclosed within a cage of relentlessly engulfing flames!

CHAPTER 10:
DUKE ESPROC REVADAC.

Roger had no idea how they hadn't already been burnt to a crisp, but by the loud roaring of the fire and the flickering tongues of flame, coming ever nearer towards them, he could tell that it wouldn't be very long at all before they were both roasted alive!

They were once again back in their bodies. Mary was still hurt and unconscious and Roger still grimly on guard, staring out at the on-coming tide of fire that was rapidly approaching them.

It was then that Mother Nature's miraculous 'Magic' and Roger's much wished for 'Wings' came to them in the most unexpected of forms. Three huge, Swooping-Rat-bat creatures came sweeping down towards them, from seemingly out of nowhere.

Two large bat-winged creatures of the night landed on the rock beside them, quickly followed by a third, from which a small dark figure gaily waved a greeting. Roger saw with a mix of both relief and disbelief, that it was the little Night Imp. Nimp was sitting astride the furry neck of the last and largest arrival. He jumped with an easy spring from his strange winged steed and then urgently called for them to quickly get onto the two awaiting Rat-bats' backs.

Nimp had not betrayed them after all - he had gone for the help that they had so desperately needed, and he had now returned with it, despite all the dangers in his way.

Roger gaped disbelievingly, as he saw that the Rat-bat, Nimp had been sitting on, transform in front of his eyes, in a bat's heart-beat. Suddenly, right before him, stood the tall, angular figure of Duke Esproc Revadac. The just recently met Tree King's Courtier and Lord of the Dark Folk!

Nimp had raced faster than the speed of night itself, through the deep shadowy reaches of the Bad Wood, to catch up with the departing Night-Folk, and particularly to find the Duke Esproc; the Lord and Master of the Dark Folk; and persuade him to come to their aid.

"Goodz eveningz, Master Roger!" Duke Esproc said, giving Roger a stiff but polite little bow.

"Pleezed to meet yooz againz; vee iz herez to 'elp; and juzz in zer nickerz of timez, I zee!"

Mary was still not able to move, but Duke Esproc effortlessly pulled her, with one bony hand, up onto the waiting Rat-bat's back. "He's definitely a lot stronger than he looks," Roger thought.

The wall of flame was now encircling them and roaring ever louder in its hot, raging frenzy. Roger could feel the battering waves of heat, radiating off the very rock they stood on, as well as scorching the soles of his feet. This rock on which they'd taken their final refuge would soon be completely overrun with fire. Then they would all be consumed: Nimp, the children and the egg; they would all be sacrificed as hapless victims to its ravenous and relentless hunger.

Unfortunately, Mary was not able to remain seated upright by herself. She kept slipping off, sliding sideways and nearly tumbling off the Rat-bat's back into the advancing flames.

Seeing this Roger and the Duke both darted to her aid and caught her before she could fall and hurt herself any further. There was no way Mary was flying off anywhere unless she regained consciousness. Roger realized they had to get Mary to stay on the Rat-bat's back. They had to bring her round somehow, just for her to be able to take off with them and escape in time.

"Vee muzz get er avake zumhowz zo she can flyz!" Duke Esproc cried out to them urgently. "Quickleez now, 'old 'er in your armz Master Roger anz I vill do vot iz nezzezzarry!"

Roger dutifully held her from behind, his arms around her waist as the Duke bent over her from the front. He seemed to be whispering something to her. Roger couldn't really see or hear what he was doing from where he stood, but whatever it was, it worked.

After a few seconds the Duke stepped back from Mary's pale, unconscious frame and all at once, Mary stirred and moaned and then sat up, looking bewilderedly all around her.

"Wh-wh-what's happenin', Roj? Where am I? What's going on?" she gasped, breathing heavily and her cheeks flushing red.

"No time to explain now, Mary," Roger answered, "we're being rescued, so just get on your Rat-bat and hold on tight, we're getting out of here right now!"

"Vee vill fly to zee top of zee Hooterz Hill," Lord Esproc told them. "Zee forest firez vill not reach youz there ant I vill ven continuez leading my peeplez to safety acrozz zee River Tymes. Zey do not like zee vater very much at allz; ant zey vill needz me!"

With that Roger jumped onto the back of his own Rat-bat steed and in the blink of a bat's eye, the Duke transformed once again into his own Rat-bat form. Nimp jumped back onto the Duke's bat-back and the three web-winged creatures leapt up into the fiery, red skies, their leather black wings madly beating, battling them up and away from the horrific cauldron of flames below.

"Easy-over or Sunny-side up, it wouldn't make a blind bit of difference now," Roger grimly thought, as he hung on to the Rat-bat's back, clinging onto its furry neck with an iron-like grip. The fiery Bad Wood fell away below them, as they headed towards the safety of Hooter's Hill.

Roger was pleased to observe that Mary still had the Dragon's Egg bulging beneath her coat. She was sitting as best she could on her Rat-bat's back. She even managed to give Roger a brief smile as they flew along, side by side for a short while.

He wasn't sure, what with the gouts of grey smoke still wafting about and it being night time; and also, the only light was that coming from the stars and flames of the forest fire behind them, but for just a moment, he thought he saw two small marks on her neck. Just like two little holes; and they seemed to be bleeding!

"Hmmm..." Roger thought, "I'd better look into that more closely, when we land, I reckon!"

All that Mary really knew at this point though, was that no matter what, she mustn't let go of the precious Dragon's Egg. She had it safely wrapped under her coat and wedged tightly between her and the rat-bat's neck, while she clung on to her curious flying steed for dear life.

"I must, I promised! I must protect the egg, I must, I promised, I promised!" she muttered to herself, over and over, as she swooped away from the cauldron of fire that was the Bad Wood.

Below them, the tree canopy swept silently by. In the darkness, though they couldn't really recognize any of the places they'd traveled through earlier that day; or was it yesterday now? Roger glumly realized that this whole area of new plants and new bugs, that he and Mary would have loved to have explored, would all be completely destroyed; all consumed in the forest fire, that was still raging its relentless way across the Bad Wood behind them.

The Rat-bats flapped tirelessly onwards, like dark shadows silhouetted against the starry sky. Soon the children could see the hazy flanks of Hooters Hill rising steadily before them, climbing free from the as yet untouched trees that surrounded it. Then, very quickly, they were once again upon the barren crown of the hill; the very place from where they'd first seen the Smoking Tree, for what seemed like half an eternity ago now.

The Duke alighted first, rapidly changing into his tall, gangly human form. Nimp jumped off his back as soon as he did so and immediately went to assist Mary. But Mary was feeling as fit as a fiddle now and leaped off from her Rat-bat steed as if she had coiled springs in her legs. Roger though, was far less buoyant, both in mood and agility.

"I don't think I'm really cut out for all this flying business, especially on these great Rat-bat thingamajigs! Still, if wishes were horses...beggars would ride!" he muttered moodily.

The Duke Esproc Revadac now stood like a statue at the brow of the hill, silently looking out, across the trees. His eyes glittering like two, pale flames in the night. The forest fire they had just escaped was still busily rampaging its way towards them. But he now faced Roger and Mary and again giving a little bow, spoke to them in his soft, clipped, but always polite manner.

"I vill be leavingz youz both 'ere. Zee Night Imp vill guide youz nowz. He knowz zee vay. I muzt returnz to my peeplez. Youz can eezily getz to zee Quaggy from here. Ant don't youz forgetz. Youz haz zee Magic Tokenz. Zo with zee Night Imp anz zee tokens, youz vill be fine!"

While Duke Esproc had been speaking though, Roger had taken a closer look at Mary's neck. And he saw it was definitely a bite. He could clearly see two small puncture holes on her neck. They were no longer bleeding, the recent trickles of blood had now dried up, but the holes were still visible. Mary had definitely been bitten... and by something very much like a Vampire!

Roger felt both alarmed and scared. The only creature he'd heard of that could change into a bat and who bit people on their necks, was a Vampire, as in all the stories of Count Dracula of Transfusionia! Could it be true? Was Duke Esproc really, just a Vampire; one of those creatures he'd read about in myths and legends, that fed on human blood and who couldn't be killed by any normal human means? Is this the creature who they had been trusting their very lives to? Despite his earlier protestations, Roger just had to know the truth.

"Excuse me' Mister, er, I mean Duke Esproc. I don't mean to be rude, but, er, erm, I mean... please excuse me, b-b-but you are, aren't you? You are, er, a V-V-Vampire, aren't you?"

The Duke immediately wheeled right around to face Roger. His face looked pale and stern. His long black cape flapped about his bony shoulders and he slowly raised a pointed finger.

"How darez youz, young zir! How darez youz? Youz again accuze meez of being zee creature of zee mythz and zee legendz! I, Duke Esproc Redavac; youz callz az some fictitious character, found only in zee lurid comic bookz and zee cheap movie picturez? I av already told youz; I am not zee zo-called Vampire. Zee Vampire, it iz zee 'orrid leettle bat who livez in zee dark caves, in zee junglez of South Ameriga that zuckz on zee bloodz of weaker animalz. I ant my kindz are of zee Dark Folkz, vee haz nothingz to do with zuch creaturez, do youz hearz me – nothingz!"

Nimp hearing the Duke's angry outburst with some alarm, immediately sprang to Roger's aid.

"Pleeze do forgives hims, yer Dark Lordship, he knowz nex to nuffinz of the wayz of any of ver Dark Folks. He really duz not meenz to be rude!"

"Harrumph!" Esproc snorted. "Vell, hiz lack of zee educationz is appallingz iz all I can zay."

"Well, if it waddles like a duck, quacks like a duck... it sounds like he's in denial to me," Roger muttered very quietly to himself, and somewhat rudely and petulantly too.

Nimp took him roughly by the arm and led him quickly off to one side. "Shhhh now, Roger; ver Duke haz exzepshonally goot hearingz!"

"Sorry, but I really don't get what the fuss is all about. What's wrong with being a Vampire anyway, if that's what you are?" Roger asked the Night Imp sulkily.

"Eet iz a long story, Roger; there iz no time to explainz to yooz now. Just accept viss pleeze. Ver Duke iz a very goot friend to 'ave! Believe this, Roger; I myzelf am of ver Dark Folks too. Do not judge us juzz by our lookz!"

"Yes, you're right, Nimp, of course," said Roger, bashfully, suddenly remembering his recent terrible attitude and behavior towards him; and all because Nimp had looked dark and different like he was something out of some silly horror movie. And actually, Nimp had behaved nothing like a monster or a demon, in reality. In fact, he had been a brave, loyal and intelligent person, and a very good one to have as a friend.

Roger turned to where the Duke was stiffly standing and gave him a low and solemn bow. Then slowly, he extended his hand and offered him a courteous handshake in apology.

"I am v-v-very sorry for my saying anything to insult you, I really am, S-s-sir." he stuttered. "I want to thank you for s-s-saving us and for, well, for everything that you've d-d-done; and for helping Mary recover and all that too, w-w-whatever that was," he finished, feeling flustered.

But the Duke bowed back and then broke into a beaming, toothy smile, his prominent pointed fangs glinting in the starry night. He then slowly took Roger's hand and shook it vigorously.

"I apolojize too, Master Roger; I voz too hasty. Yooz ver not to knowz." He signaled to his Rat-bat companions and then bowed toward Nimp and Mary. "Ant nowz vee muzt leave. Vee vill all meetz againz vun day ant I vill alvays do vot I can to azzist youz. Keep zee Egg zafe, ant fare zee vell!"

The Duke quickly transformed into a bat and then the three Rat-bats, flew up into the night, steadily flapping northwards, back to his people and the relative safety of the River Tymes.

"Ant vere iz no needz to fangz me; it iz I oo fangz youz!" the Duke enigmatically called back. Then the three shadowy bat-shapes had vanished into the night and were gone.

"Vell, now vee must be on our wayz too!" called out Nimp. "Vee must get yoos safely downs to ver River Quaggy and on yer wayz home."

"OK, Nimp," Roger replied, rather red-faced, "b-b-but I just want to say one thing to you. I'm very s-s-sorry for not trusting you and thinking that you were evil and had betrayed us and had just left us to die. I didn't think. And I didn't really know you, b-b-but I made up my mind anyway and decided you were bad for no good reason."

"Applejoozes acksepted!" Nimp replied, with a broad smile. "Ver black skinz duzn't meanz ver black hearts now duz it, eh?" And with that they made their way together, united as friends, over towards the southern edge of the hilltop, to begin their descent to the River Quaggy.

"So, is he a Vampire then?" asked Mary of Roger quietly, as he walked alongside her.

"Well, not as we think of them," Roger replied. "He's definitely a friend though," he added.

"Well, I feel wonderful!" Mary laughed exultantly. "I feel really alive and like I could run at least ten marathons, one after the other, even!"

"Yes, yoos probbly canz, fer nowz," Nimp butted in, "but ver spell vill vear off after a whilez. Ant I must warnz yoos, Mary; yoos vill probbly 'av at least vun or even more of ver Dark Folk's 'Super-powerz,' as yoos silly humanz callz zem."

"Oh really, that's great!" cried Mary, very happy to hear that. "What ones will I have?"

"I vould zay vat yoos 'ave ver sooper-strength and ver sooper-dumb luck!" Nimp chuckled.

The three had now walked their way over the brow of the hill and began their descent, down toward the distant, squiggly line of the River Quaggy. Faint reddish slithers of the river briefly appeared, where the forest fire had already encroached upon it eastwards of them,

Roger realized that they had to get down as fast as possible before the fire caught up with them and surrounded the foot of Hooter's Hill. He looked back towards the way they'd flown and saw that the forest fire was definitely spreading fast, sending out pseudopodia-like arms of snaking red flame towards the banks of the river.

He could see it wouldn't be too long before the fire would encircle the whole of Hooter's Hill. But if they didn't delay, he judged, they'd still be able to cross it in time.

"Let's get a move on," he called out, "we've got to beat those flames before they cut us off!"

Then, without warning, Roger stopped in his tracks and let out a very loud "Ow!"

He had just felt a sharp pain in the top of his leg. He quickly investigated there, delving into his trouser pocket, right where the hanky with the Magic Tokens was. He found that one of them, a small, sharp tooth, had somehow gotten free of the hanky and pierced his leg. He could feel it; the little tooth-token had somehow actually bitten him!

He now heard the Duke Esproc's voice, telepathically echoing in his head, chanting to him: "Ver wingz of ver Dark Folkz make ver light workz of ver dark deedz – ver lighter vay are!"

"What the Archimedes Screw does that mean?" Roger exclaimed, puzzled. "And why has a magic token kicked in right now, there's no immediate, life-threatening danger, is there?" he added worriedly.

"Hey, hold on," Mary called, "I've got a sort of bat-radar sense too I think, and it's tingling. There is definitely something, and it's dangerous and getting nearer, but I don't know what it is!"

Roger didn't answer though; he couldn't, he was too busy with the very strange changes that were happening to him. He felt a cold, prickly energy spreading through his veins. Then his back began to itch, right between the shoulder blades, just where he couldn't reach. He twisted and he turned, but he just couldn't get to it. His back was now burning and starting to bubble and boil, and he felt his shirt and jacket ripping and tearing.

Duke Esproc's magical tooth-token was definitely taking effect!

"Oh! Your back, Roger, it's your back – look, you're growing wings!" Mary screamed at him.

And it was true. After but a few seconds more, two black stumps had pushed their way out from his back. Then they steadily grew larger; and soon they were unfurling as a magnificent pair of leathery, black bat wings!

"By Socrates Socks! So that's what Duke Esproc meant!" Roger grinned. "These will definitely make my work a lot lighter!"

He flapped the wings a few times, getting the feel of his new and wonderful appendages.

"By Galileo's Galloping Gumdrops, I believe I can really fly!" Roger exclaimed.

And so, he did. Hesitantly at first, but then with increasing confidence, he flapped his black Bat-wings and briefly hovered over Mary and Nimp, then with a bump, landed beside them.

"Wow!" said Mary, "that's incredible, Roger!"

"The Magic Token, the tooth; it b-b-bit me," he told them in explanation. "The Duke Esproc's magical gift, it's been activated somehow; but I have no idea why!"

"I do!" Mary cried, suddenly shouting in alarm and pointing in horror behind them.

"Look, up there," she cried, "right behind us, we're under attack again!"

CHAPTER 11:
ATTACK OF THE DEATH WORMS!

Roger looked and could hardly believe what he saw. The bald head of Hooter's Hill was growing hair!

At least that was what it looked like. The area of the hill that they'd been standing on was now sprouting hundreds of strange grub-like creatures. But as they came up through the dirt, Roger could see they were more like elongated slugs than grubs. They were about a foot long but were probably twice that, depending on how much of their length was still underground.

They waved about, eerily silhouetted against the starry night sky, their sickly, pale bodies undulating from side to side as if they were sensing the air and sniffing out their intended prey. Which was of course, exactly what they were doing.

"Veez are ver deadly Death Worms!" Nimp exclaimed. "Vay come from vot ver Dark Folks call ver Maggot Cavernz, deep beneath ver Northern Seaz. The Fire-Worm Lord must 'ave sent themz to interzept us."

"By Faraday's Furry Face! He hasn't given up then. I would have thought the explosion of Mavis would've put paid to him, at least for a while anyway." Roger fervently swore.

"Ver Fire-Worms are all but indestructible, Roger. Ezpeshally ven vay are at ver Erf's Core. Here though vay are near ver surface, ant vay get weaker. It iz zed that sunlight can kill vem if vay are expozed to it too long."

"Shame we don't have any sunlight to hand then, to deal with them isn't it?" Roger replied.

"Yes, but ver Death Worms, vay 'ave ver same weakness," Nimp answered, ignoring Roger's sarcasm. "Vay are blind but vay can smell ant can sense their preyz by their antennae vat pickz up any radiation disturbanzez from a great distance. Vay vill keeps awayz from anything that iz too bright or too hot for vemz."

"Good to know!" Mary interjected, "But what are we going to do? As Roj said we don't have any sunshine to bless their horrible hides with, now do we!"

"Here they come!" Roger shouted, seeing the first of the Death Worms slithering fully out of their holes and making their way towards them. "Hooter's Hill is losing its Hair!"

He saw that the Death Worms were much larger than the minion worms that had attacked them earlier in Mavis's Cavern; when fully out of their holes they were at least two foot long. They were all the same deathly white color and glistened with an oily slug-slime, that trailed behind them just as with normal Erf slugs you'd find in your own back garden.

"Whatever 'appenz, do not touch ver Death Worm's slime, it is a deadly, toxic acid ant vill kill anything it touches in secondz!"

"Again. Good to know. Let's get out of here fast!" Mary exclaimed, calling back to them, her super strength enabling her to run speedily ahead of them.

But the steepness of the hill meant they couldn't run down it too quickly or they'd just fall and tumble on down and probably break their necks. But Roger and Nimp followed on after Mary the best that they could. Nimp hopping down the hill with rapid, rabbit-like jumps and with Roger taking long bounds and leaps that his new Bat wings helped him perform.

"I could fly and carry you, Nimp, we'd make better time then, OK?" Roger kindly offered.

"No vank youz, Master Roger. I vill be right behind youz, don't vurry," Nimp answered him.

But the Death Worms were catching them up. The Egg-bearers had barely made their way over the brow of the steep hill, when the vile, sluggy creatures had first appeared, but now they were slithering their slimy, vermicular trails rapidly down upon them, at an alarming speed.

"Oh, fidgety fiddlesticks!" Mary swore, looking behind her. "I can outrun them I think, you can outfly them Roger, but what about you, Nimp? Don't be silly, let Roger help you."

"Oh, very vell, I vill fly a short vayz wiv you, but pleeze be carefulz, Roger. You iz not very egzperienzed at ver flyingz yet ant I don't like to fly vat much anyvay!" Nimp reluctantly agreed.

With that said, the Night Imp allowed Roger to grab hold of him and they swooped up into the air just yards in front of the advance rank of the Death Worms, now swarming down upon them.

Roger found he was more able to catch up with Mary now. Though the added weight of the Night Imp didn't help much at all. It wasn't so much his weight though, but more from Roger being so unskilled at flying, and keeping his balance and going in a straight line when doing so; especially when he had a somewhat nervous Night Imp hanging from his waist.

But he was still able to spread his bat wings and with some hasty flaps, dart away from the Death Worm's deadly reach. Their jets of acid slime were coming at him fast and furiously though and he found he had to dodge and weave about in the air, like a veteran aerial acrobat.

"Talk about a steep learning curve!" he grimly muttered to himself, as he avoided yet another barrage of poisonous spit flying towards him.

But these Death Worms were being guided by a powerful and cunning mind, being directly controlled by a Fire-Worm Lord of the Core. Roger gasped as he saw they now began to fuse together. Their slimy slug-bodies sliding on top of each other as they slithered down the hill.

This had the immediate effect of creating several waves of Death Worm clusters, that rose up ever higher, as they flowed down the hillside. Roger soon found out why they were doing this though, as the nearest wave rose up right behind him and let loose a deadly barrage of spurts.

Roger barely had time to bank to one side and avoid all the vile splatter. But more waves were forming now, as the long, slug-like bodies of the Death Worms slid on over each other and fused themselves into one deadly rising form.

"These super-slugs have developed their foot fringes, so they act as long suction pads that keep them locked together, very clever that is!" he thought. "Well, no time for Entomology right now; we've got to get away from these filthy blighters!"

But the Death Worms were getting better every second at coordinating their attack waves and at the accuracy of their firing too. A sizzling blast of goo went flying by in front of him which he just avoided by banking sharply to the left, but another wave rose on that side, unseen by him, and fired yet another blast of acid slime, this time catching Roger on one of his bat wings.

He immediately felt the leathery material of his wing starting to shrivel and to develop holes from the burning acid. And now his flying became extremely erratic, any moment, another blast would finish him and Nimp off for good.

But Nimp had other ideas! As he dangled inelegantly from Roger's trousers, he managed to deftly let off a small cloud of 'Dark' behind Roger's back. This covered the damaged wing and had the much-needed effect of dampening down the burning acid-slime. He then twisted and threw another much larger 'Dark' bomb into a nearby Death Worm Wave, looming up at them, sending it crashing down into confusion in the choking black fog that swiftly enveloped it.

Roger though was in trouble. He found the harder he flapped his bat wings the more unstable he became in the air. After a few seconds of careening about and nearly plunging into the hillside, he finally managed a semi-controlled crash landing.

Nimp scurried over to Roger who lay dazed on the ground. "Quick, Roger, getz up," he yelled. "We haz to getz avay, ver Death Worms will be onto us any zecond!"

Roger groaned and pulled himself up. He could see that the front guard of the attacking Death Worms had already rallied and was emerging out of Nimp's black fog towards them. He took stock and steadied himself, flapping his Bat wings and testing their usefulness.

"I'll be alright, Nimp, I think my wings are too, but we'll have to keep closer to the ground. Look, there's an outcrop of rocks down there, near where Mary is, let's try for them!"

Nimp grabbed hold of Roger around the waist once more and they took off. This time though Roger could only manage low-level, long glides down the hillside, several times nearly losing control and almost crashing into the scrubby ground.

The Death Worms weren't waiting around though; they now doubled their efforts and came slithering right behind, in their hundreds in wave after wave. But Nimp managed to let off a few more of his 'Dark' bombs, bouncing behind him, as they made their way down the slope, much like a bouncing bomb themselves in fact, towards the rocky outcrop that loomed ever nearer.

Mary had reached some way further down the hill, beyond the outcrop of rocks, but now she stopped to see what was happening with her companions. She felt horrified, and somewhat guilty too, at seeing them so far behind her. She felt caught between using her new super strength for running on to the Quaggy and saving herself and the Dragon's Egg or turning back and doing whatever she could to save her friends.

Mary only hesitated for a second though. Roger and Nimp needed her help; there was no way she could leave them to such a grisly fate as being smothered in a blanket of toxic slug-slime!

She was halfway back to them when disaster struck!

Nimp was hit. The Night Imp had been hanging on to Roger and hurling his Dark Bombs as best he could. Roger was desperately bouncing along, taking long, weaving glides down the hill and trying to keep his balance as he did so, and he was definitely getting better at it.

But the Death Worms were learning too,

Two Waves of the slimy creatures had formed on either side of the fleeing duo and were actively herding them like sheep into a pen. They were trying to trap Roger and Nimp in a pincer movement. Nimp tried to warn Roger, but as he cried out one of the waves of super-slugs veered towards them and fired. Roger tried his best to avoid the slime blast, but not fast enough!

Nimp went careening over the stony ground, rolling towards the rocks. And then lay still just several yards in front of them. His back and one arm were covered with the silvery, icky goo but he wasn't conscious now to feel the pain.

Roger quickly landed next to him in a running stumble. The waves of Death Worms were converging right in front of him and Nimp, and growing ever higher. Roger could see that they obviously intended to pour themselves over them and so totally overwhelm and drown them in a fatal cascade of their toxic bodies and slug-slime.

As they surged ever higher, Roger grabbed hold of Nimp and dragged him the short distance to the rocks behind them. But he realized that these wouldn't be any defense in themselves. The flood of looming Death Worms was about to crash down on them any second and they'd be done for!

"Use the Blue Dragon Fire, Roger. Quick, it's your only chance!" Mary screamed out to him.

"Of course!" Roger thought. "If I can muster some, at least it'll delay the inevitable!"

He tried to clear his mind and just concentrate on creating the protective bubble of blue fire. He knew he had to be quick, but within a gnat's whisker, he did it. Just as the first of the torrent of slugs and their slime fell on their heads, the quivering, blue bubble formed around them.

Roger knelt beside the unconscious Nimp and kept the bubble of blue Dragon Fire sparkling above their heads. And the fountain of Death Worms came cascading down upon them, and very soon completely covering the blue sphere so that all Roger could see was the silvery slime and the disgusting bellies of the scores of slithering slugs sliding down its sides.

And then Roger realized. "What about Mary... and the Egg? Oh, by Jumping James Joules! Mary is still out there, unprotected!"

And to add unwanted fuel to the fire, Roger could see that the Slug's acid slime was eating away at the blue fire-bubble's surface. He had absolutely no idea how long it would last!

But Mary wasn't helpless though. She sprinted up the hill to the rocks where Roger valiantly concentrated on keeping the protective bubble burning about him and the still unconscious Nimp.

On her way up she grabbed hold of two sinewy, sapling trees, wrenching them from out the stony ground with the benefit of her super strength. Then she launched herself upon the fallen Death Worms that lay squirming in a thick, oozing pile all around the rocks and the small, blue protective dome that contained her two friends.

She then set about the slugs, whirling the saplings in front of her like two whirring propellers, doing her Whirling Dervish trick again, but this time at super speed and using her super strength.

Using the trees like spinning blades, Mary soon sliced and slashed the Death Worms away from the wavering bubble, the hurricane-like force of the whirlwind she created, safely keeping any of their poisonous slimes away from her as well.

But she knew that she couldn't keep it up forever. There were just too many of them and more were still coming. She stood in front of the rocks and prepared herself for another onslaught of the Death Worms.

"If they form more of those waves then they'll get me for sure!" she thought desperately.

But Roger could see too. The blue bubble now being clear of slugs and his heart turned to lead as he saw Mary a little way in front of him, standing bravely, legs akimbo, awaiting to do battle.

"Don't stay there, Mary!" he yelled at her. "They'll get you for sure. Quick, I'll lower the blue-fire bubble and you can get in with us. Nimp could do with your help too!"

Mary looked around and saw Roger on his knees straining with the effort, sweat and dirt smearing his face and the unconscious Night Imp lying beside him. She realized that Roger was right. She'd never manage to hold off such a horde of vile, slimy fiends by herself.

"OK, Roj. You're right. Lower away."

With that, she dropped the saplings and turned and dived across the rock and threw herself into Roger's arms, just as he stood up and let the blue bubble disintegrate.

They stood there together, momentarily stunned, but then Nimp groaned and Mary went to his side to offer what aid she could. Roger immediately raised the protective blue-fire bubble again. And just in time, as the Death Worms were now once more upon them.

"Oh, flamin' finkle-flies!" Mary exclaimed angrily. "That's just great, now we're all caught an' cozy... an' trapped!"

"Better than being under that lot!" Roger answered her gravely, pointing to the wave of Death Worms building up in front of the rocks once more and smothering the ground where Mary had just been standing.

The Night Imp was now coming around, sitting up and rubbing his shoulder. Mary helped him peel off the hardening slime from where it had congealed on his skin. Nimp was of hardy stuff and able to withstand such burns and wounds far better than a Human could.

"Look, there are gaps between these rocks," Roger pointed out, "maybe we can wend our way through them. A bit of the way down anyway. And they'll help keep these acid spitting vermin off us too," he added.

"OK. Lead on, Sir Knight," Mary sighed wearily, helping Nimp to his feet.

"Are vay ztill afterz us ven?" Nimp enquired, somewhat groggily.

"Yes, they are, so keep moving, alright!" Roger replied testily and taking the lead through a nearby deep cleft between two of the rocks. More of the Death Worms still tried to fall on them, but a lot fewer than before and those that did appear just slid off the magical blue fire bubble.

The three friends moved as quickly and quietly as they could, winding in and out between the rocks but soon the area of the hill where the rocks were dwindled completely away.

Before them stretched just plain open hillside with very little vegetation. There were a few bits of scrub and bush and the odd sapling or wind-tortured, small tree, but nothing else to stop a torrent of flesh-hungry, killer slugs.

"Oh, Shivering Schroedinger! We'll never make it, trying to run down that!" Roger hissed.

"Then what are we going to do?" Mary asked, looking glumly down the exposed slope. "I'm not strong enough to run with the both of you. And you can't fly properly and not while carrying Nimp anyway. And I don't think Nimp's Dark Bombs are going to help us get away either!"

"And look, behind us," Roger gasped, "the Death Worms are flooding through the rocks anyway. There's no way back now!"

And it was true. The Death Worms had learnt to control their flow and move together like many rippling rivers of slime, flowing through all the rock's crevices and cracks.

"Quick!" Roger cried. "Climb on top of the rocks. The Death Worms will have to collect back together and reform again to get at us up there."

The three Egg-bearers followed Roger's lead and started scrambling up the large pitted rock they were standing next to. When they reached the top Roger saw that it was like a plateau of rock up there that you could move across as long as you chose a workable route, jumping across cracks and canyons that were jumpable. Roger hesitated, unsure as to which way to go.

The Death Worms continued flowing like tight-packed, deadly rivers below them. But Mary stepped forward, her super strength and agility coming to the fore when rock climbing and jumping across twisting cracks in the rocky floor.

"Follow me, you two. If we get in the middle, on top of this rocky outcrop, then these things will at least have a harder time reaching us, right?"

"Right!" Roger agreed.

Soon the three of them stood on as near the dead center of the rocks as Mary could navigate. She had somehow found a route that even Roger, with his great distaste of heights, found that he could safely manage.

"What now?" he asked her breathlessly.

"I don't know, Roger. Maybe you'll be brilliant and come up with something!" she answered.

The Death Worms had reached the other end of the area of rocks and were now fully aware that their prey had not continued on down the hill. It didn't take them (or the powerful mind that was controlling them), very long to deduce where they were most likely to be.

Soon several towers of the long slimy creatures were forming as they interwove their supple, soft bodies, like growing, plaited ropes, reaching upwards towards the top of the rocks, where Roger, Mary, and Nimp stood helplessly waiting.

Roger was aching and trembling. And not just with fear. He was becoming increasingly aware that his ability to keep the magical blue fire burning was all that was in the way of their being destroyed once and for all.

But there had to be a way. Mavis had said, there was always a way. And the Tree King and Mother Nature herself, the Goddess Gaia. They all had told him, in their own ways, that there was always a solution to any problem.

"There must be a way out of this. There just must be!" he muttered grimly to himself.

Mary could see that Roger was in some distress. She took hold of his hand and squeezed it. "It's all right, Roj. None of this is your fault. I think you're the bravest and most valiant knight Irritant I know!" She smiled at him. "You're a true warrior if ever there was one!"

Roger looked at her, blankly at first, but then his eyes widened and brightened.

He'd just had an amazing idea.

CHAPTER 12:
MORGRAVE'S REVENGE.

"I think there's something I can do Mary. It's our only chance anyway!"

"What on Erf's that then?" she answered, surprised but curious. "And whatever it is you better be flippin' flapjacks quick about it. Coz look, we've got unwelcome company again!"

And it was true, the Death Worms had reached the top of the rocks and were now slithering purposefully towards them, from all directions. Everywhere Roger looked he saw the foul slug-worms moving across the uneven rocky-roof, leaving their silvery slime-trails behind them.

They were slowly and surely being completely surrounded.

"Right, well, it's simple, Mary. The best form of defense is to attack... and it's about Tesla's Toe-nail's Time that we started fighting back. Running away isn't going to win this battle!"

"What! Are you mad? How are you planning to do that Roger?" Mary squealed with shock. "Oh, please don't do anything boyishly bold and foolishly fatal. Pleeease!"

Roger could tell that Mary wasn't being sarcastic, she was scared. But he had no intention of just throwing his life away. And anyway, if this didn't work, they were dead and done for by the look of the slimy, army of Death Worms slithering ever nearer.

"Look, I'll have to lower the blue bubble to do this, so get ready and run for it after I do! There's no time to explain. You and Nimp be ready though when I say."

"OK, Roj. I tr-trust you. But whatever you do, please be careful," she murmured, anxiously crossing her fingers.

The first of the Death Worms were just a few yards away so it was now or never.

Roger took a deep breath and let the magical blue fire bubble disintegrate, and as it did so he stepped through its last wavering sparkles and raised his arms in front of him as if holding a large, invisible object between his palms. He screwed his face in concentration, this time focusing on creating an entirely different sort of fireball.

This was Roger's first attempt at conjuring and using Red Dragon Fire. He had realized that just hiding under the blue fire bubble or continually trying to just run away, wasn't going to save them. He had to go on the offensive and that meant using a serious weapon. And the best weapon he could think of to exterminate slugs and such with, was hot, searing fire.

He had remembered how Mavis had dropped her blue fire bubble in order to go on the offensive against the Trydra and he realized that he could probably do the same. The only problem was he'd never done it before, so he just had to steel himself and swallow his fear and do his best. If he failed, they were all dead anyway.

He stood up, legs apart and arms outstretched, picturing the kind of heat wavelength he now needed. Then the space between his palms began to crackle and then spark with red and white lightning-like flashes, making his hands and arms tingle. But somehow the flame was unable to hurt him. He could feel it course through his body and up his arms.

The Death Worms were nearly upon him now and there were more coming to either side of him as well as from behind him. Roger gritted his teeth and conjured the hottest flame he could think of and soon a ball of writhing, red fire appeared between his hands.

The pulsating globe of ruby-red flame grew ever hotter and brighter by the second. But he didn't even have a second left.

The Death Worms were rising-up once again, forming a great wave that intended to pour over him and his friends, scorching and suffocating them in their acid slime. Roger knew that in the very next second they'd all be beyond help or... his firebomb tactic would have worked.

He balanced the large globe of sizzling flame between his hands and then with a great grunt and a shove he hurled it out straight into the mass of Death Worms looming above him.

The Red 'Flame Bomb' exploded and hundreds of hot forked-tongues of fire screamed and sizzled their way throughout the sluggy mass, immediately burning the Worms to a crisp!

Roger could hardly believe it. The Death Worms could do nothing against the ravaging red flames. They all became tortured and twisted carcasses and then as the heat radiated through them, charred and lumpy puddles of dark, sticky goo, all congealing together into a large, mutual pool of steaming, Death Worm carnage.

"It's worked! Quick; run now, I've cleared a way through!" he yelled to Mary and Nimp. "I'll bring up the rear and blast as many of these things as I can."

Mary and Nimp didn't need telling twice and set off across the rocks and back onto the hillside, heading downhill as fast as they could go.

Roger realized that he could attack more of the Death Worms if he was airborne and so flapped his great Bat Wings and launched himself into the air. His damaged Bat Wing had already begun to miraculously repair itself and he found he could swoop and hover over the rocks and aim his deadly fireballs a lot more easily now. Not having Nimp hanging from his trousers was a great help too though.

He conjured another three large balls of sizzling red flame, one after the other, hurling them into the last waves of Death Worms that were still remaining. He floated above the rock like an avenging Angel of Death, his bat-wings fully unfurled and casting the foul demons of Slugdom into the smoking pits of Hell.

Soon all the Death Worms had been incinerated and Roger lowered his arms and breathed a sigh of relief. He no longer needed to rely on his ability to be a Human Flame-thrower.

He flapped his way across the rocks, following the fleeing Mary and Nimp. He had felt elated and full of unbridled power for a short while there, but now he began to feel deflated and also, he had a dizzying headache from all his exertions. And his wings felt very heavy and cumbersome and he was starting to feel quite unwell and disoriented.

"Oh, by James Joule's Jumpers, I wasn't really ready for that at all!" he thought to himself sourly, groaning and near to throwing up.

As he flew on and hopped down the hill his mind suddenly exploded with the thunder of a Fire-Worm Lord bellowing incessantly in his head and this time it wasn't Lord Morgrave.

This voice was blacker and even more powerful and menacing than Morgrave's was, and was angrily roaring, taunting and confusing him. He could hardly see where he was going.

"Do not flee, little Humdrum; do not fly. You know it is futile! Just wait there for me and you will soon pay for your feeble crimes. I will give you peace and justice will be served!"

Roger couldn't fly properly no matter how hard he tried. He tumbled dizzily to the ground, weak and exhausted, skidding across the barren hillside and rolling in a tangle of arms, legs, and bat wings. He started to violently retch, now feeling very ill indeed. And his head was hot and swollen like it was being slowly filled with molten lead.

Mary and Nimp saw Roger was in trouble and began to raced back up the hill to help him. But as they came close, they too were suddenly struck to the ground by Morgrim's fierce Mental bellows, as several more waves of white-hot pain went coursing through their heads.

"It iz Morgrim – Morgrave's twin brother who iz doingz vis!" Nimp cried out.

"What? Morgrave has a twin!" Mary groaned, sitting slumped on the ground and clutching her temples tightly between her hands. "I can't stand it. Oh, Thunderation! How can we make him stop, Nimp? He seems even stronger than King Morgrave was!"

But then all at once the Fire Worm's mental barrage suddenly stopped... all became calm and quiet. But Roger had a sneaky suspicion that this was just the calm before the storm!

Mary and Nimp picked themselves up and helped Roger onto his feet. They stood together, blinking away the pain and dusting themselves down and preparing to flee down the hill once again. But the ground beneath their feet gave a sudden shake and then another and then a great rumbling noise filled the air.

Roger looked up at the top of the hill and rubbed at his eyes in disbelief.

"Isn't that the head of a Fire-Worm Lord, coming out the very top of the Hill up there? That can't be Morgrave, can it? Mavis said he was crippled and blinded! That must be this Morgrim chap, this twin brother of his."

The three companions stood transfixed in horror, as the top of Hooter's Hill exploded. Great gouts of flame and boiling columns of smoke rose high into the air. And the sound of the eruption hit them just as the ground also buckled and cracked under their feet with yet another tremendous erf-quake, tearing right through the flanks of Hooter's Hill.

The top of Hooter's Hill was blowing up in one gigantic flaming volcanic eruption and the Fire-Worm Lord, Morgrim. raised himself slowly up from out of the reeking cauldron of fiery magma that now bubbled over the newly formed crater's rim.

Roger gasped in shock as he saw above him, the huge, bloated body of the deadly Fire-Worm Lord. And he could tell that this was a different one. This one was bigger and longer, and felt even more powerful, especially when it came to the power of the mind.

"Oh, viz iz terriblez!" cried Nimp. "King Morgrave must hav zent for hiz twin bruvver, ver Lord Morgrim! Quick, vee must fly, it iz said vat he iz even more cruelz and powerfulz and cunningz van Morgrave iz!"

"By Faradays Furry Face! Not another Fire-Worm Lord!" exclaimed Roger in disgust. "Why can't they just leave us alone? What's wrong with these creatures anyway; they have their lovely hot Core to play in, don't they, and no one's bothering them about that, are they?"

Mary and Nimp didn't answer him. There was nothing left to say or do... but run!

Lord Morgrim, the evil twin brother of Morgrave, now reared his ugly head, bellowing and glaring down at them. He opened his great maw wide and sent out wave after wave of head-pounding, mind-mushing sonic-booms that came crashing down upon their heads.

His huge, red and black bulk swayed high over the new volcano's crater, like some gigantic prehistoric reptile. A cross between a slithering fat Python Snake and a gigantic armored, razor toothed Croco-dile, but this 'Croco-Snake' was easily a hundred feet long!

The three of them were thrown violently to the ground, as sonic booms shattered the rocks all around. Then the Erf violently shook with the tremors from yet another bone-shaking erf-quake; possibly an aftershock from the initial volcanic eruption, Roger thought.

It was now impossible for them to stand on their feet, let alone run.

Nimp though quickly acted to protect them from Morgrim's continued barrage of deadly sonic booms. As he fell to the ground, he deftly threw out a large cloud of his magical 'dark' all around them. Immediately, the loud booms dulled down to a muted background thumping and thudding. Like they'd been suddenly cocooned in dark cotton wool.

As Lord Morgrim wallowed in the fiery cauldron of the volcanic crater high above them, large seething globs of magma spilled over the rim. Now several rivers of steaming, hot lava made their snaking ways relentlessly towards them.

"Oh no! Not more boiling lava being flung at us!" cried Roger, in indignation and dismay.

But Morgrim had at least ceased his sonic booms for a while, now sensing his prey was somehow protected from them. He instead lunged forward, intent on bringing his bulk down upon them to squash them flat, like the meaningless and measly bugs he thought they were.

"Quickleez! You must fly, Roger, before it iz too late!" yelled Nimp.

Roger and Mary picked themselves up and started running, as best they could, down the hillside. But before they could really get going, Nimp cried out to them urgently.

"No, no, no! I meanz you musst fly, fly, really fly! Yooz yor wingz, Roger!"

"Oh, right!" Roger exclaimed. "Of course,... silly me! My wings! They've regenerated!"

And with that, he snapped open his bat wings and once more launched himself into the air.

"Grab onto me as I go by," he yelled to Mary, and then came gliding in a tight curve, around to where she stood waiting, still tightly clutching the dragon's egg under her coat.

Mary quickly grabbed hold of Roger's waist as he swooped by, nearly bringing him crashing to the ground with her extra weight. But he valiantly beat his bat wings with all his might and managed to steady himself in the air once again.

Now the snarling and threatening tones of Lord Morgrim exploded in their minds once again. He was speaking to them all, booming in their heads telepathically.

"So, you would dare connive with that weak-willed, winged-worm Sivam Sivad, would you? You'd dare to harm my brother, would you? Well, now you will pay for your foolish disrespect and insolence. You pitiful Humdrums and that puny putrid Egg you carry will be utterly destroyed and my regal brother will have his due revenge!"

But before Morgrim, or anyone else, could say a further word, Roger suddenly heard another second voice, blasting loudly in his head.

This was indeed the blind and now totally insane King Morgrave, raving and raging to his brother Lord Morgrim. *"That's right, my loyal* brother, we'll smash 'em all; we'll smash an' we'll smear 'em all over the rocks – but leave me that Dragon's Egg, I'm coming, do you hear? I'm on my way, it must be me that destroys the Egg, it is my right - to end the line of Sivad, forever! It must be me! Do you hear?"

Lord Morgrim was momentarily stunned. How could his brother be so idiotically stupid? Didn't he know how badly hurt he now was? What on Erf could he be thinking, had he lost his mind? He then quickly scanned his brother's mind and realized that yes, King Morgrave had indeed lost it, totally!

His rage had consumed him. He was blind to all reason. All he now cared about was the utter destruction of the two Humdrum children and the Royal Dragon's Egg.

Nothing else mattered to him whatsoever!

Roger was also shocked. This was absolutely terrible news; now they had two deadly Fire-Worm Lords to deal with. He calmed and steeled himself though, despite the sick knot in his stomach grinding away like a cement mixer.

He continued to glide with Mary clumsily and as silently as he could down the hill. The Fire-Worms continued their mind argument as the children slowly made their descent, bumping and gliding close to the ground, with the Night Imp darting along as fast as he could not far behind them.

"Morgrave go back!" Morgrim mentally commanded. "You are not well and I as your twin and brother will see to these meddling fools on your behalf. I will bring the Egg to you, for you to destroy personally, but you must remain under the Erf. You are already weakened. You know our kind cannot last very long on the surface, under all this deadly sky and air!"

"But I am the King!" hissed Morgrave, indignantly. "It is not your turn to command!"

"Yes, brother," Morgrim replied as patiently as he could, "but we both will have many more turns wearing the crown; if we now follow the Core-Law as prescribed by the ancient ones so many eons ago! Trust me, brother;

there are plans in progress, even now as we argue, that will ensure our complete dominion over the entire Erf; these must not be jeopardized!"

"But the winged-worm blinded me, Morgrim; I know of no such plans and I must have my revenge, do you hear me?" Morgrave howled, blind to any reason, as well as to any sight.

"I know, brother, I know; and you will, I promise. But it is my duty as your twin and as your royal brother. Each must aid the other during their thousand years' term of Kingship. You well know this! For if one is deposed or destroyed, then the other can no longer take his turn on the throne. Your current glorious reign is nearly ended, Morgrave. It is vital that you see your Kingship through to full term, so there will be others for us both – so heed me now. Do not throw away our chance of ruling the Erf's Core, and even more, again!"

Morgrim's self-serving but persuasive argument and mollifying tone seemed to have done the trick, at least for the time being. There were no more howls of discontent from Morgrave.

Roger could only hear the muffled mutters and grumbled growling and grinding of teeth, telepathically emanating from the irate and tortured King Morgrave, as he restlessly seethed, nearby but unseen in the magma pool, deep in the heart of the newly erupted volcano.

Despite his horrific wounds and blindness, Morgrave had managed to drag and burrow his way out of Mavis's shattered cavern and had somehow tracked them and his brother here.

Roger was finding himself becoming more and more familiar with using telepathy now. He found he could hear and view any other telepathic creature's senses just so long as they didn't block him from doing so. As he flapped along, bumping Mary as little as possible on the ground, he became very curious and dared himself a quick look; wanting to experience seeing through the eyes of the mad and badly wounded Morgrave.

This, of course, was a big mistake!

Morgrave immediately sensed the mental intrusion and screamed out his blind hatred with Erf shattering fury. He grew increasingly hotter and hotter, turning a livid red and purple with rage. The magma pool all around him hissed and steamed and then boiled over and exploded, spewing a fountain of fiery lava up the volcano's throat and high into the night air.

The volcano's crater now cracked in several places around its rim, spilling out even more of the deadly rivers of molten lava, that snaked hissing and spitting their fiery way, down the hillside, flowing relentlessly on towards the children and the Night Imp.

"Calm down, Morgrave; further mindless chaos and futile destruction are of no use to us, trust me, my brother, I will see that you get your re- venge," Morgrim telepathed as coolly as he could, trying yet again to placate his insane sibling. *"I need to concentrate on the hunt and the kill, for your honor, and with no further delay or distraction. These puny Over-Erf vermin are even now trying to slip away and save their sorry skins!"*

"Get me that Dragon's Egg then; Bring me the Egg, do you hear!" Mor- grave screamed, almost choking himself with the uncontrollable ha- tred that was still boiling his black blood.

While the twin Fire-Worm Lords had been busy arguing with each other, the three fleeing Egg bearers had done their best to get further down the hillside. Roger, with Mary hanging on for dear life and poor Nimp, leaping along behind them like a dark and darting skinny rabbit.

The tree-line was still quite some way below them though and Morgrim had pulled all of his long lizardish bulk over the crater's rim and was now clawing and sliding his way rapidly down towards them.

And Roger saw he was making his way along a useful long crack that radiated out from the volcano's crater in their direction. And he was again using his sonic booms on them; sending rock-splitting waves ahead of him that created one long, zig-zag crack, even further down through the rocky slope. Morgrim rode along this crack, some- what protected on his flanks, from the (to him) deadly openness of the night sky above.

Then Mary cried out with a loud yelp of pain. But not from Morgrim's sonic booms. Nimp had managed to keep his bubbles of dark billowing about them.

"Roger, look, look! Below us, there's more of those fire-worm minions! They're breaking out through the hillside everywhere. They're trying to bite us. Can't you go any higher, Roj?"

"S-s-sorry, Mary, I just can't," Roger replied, breathlessly. "I can b-b-barely keep flying; anyway, you're the one with super strength you know, not me!"

Morgrim was getting closer now. *"Do not resist me!"* he boomed. *"Surrender the Egg and I will spare you your worthless lives!"* he lied, as his fuming bulk came ever nearer.

Then Roger saw ahead of them another rocky outcrop; jutting out from the side of the hill.

"Look, over there, Mary, we'll head for that rocky shelf. At least those fire-worm minions won't be able to get at us so easily there."

"Stop!" screamed Morgrim, using all the compelling power of his telepathic mind-control that he could muster. *"Stop now and surrender, I command it!"*

Roger felt as if a great hand had held him by the collar and wrenched him backward!

But the valiant Night Imp immediately threw out another cloud of his 'dark' between them and Morgrim. Once again, the cloud of 'dark' dampened and dissipated the power and energy of the Worm Lord's commands. Roger had hesitated for a few flaps of his bat wings but was now able to flap onwards and make his way to the rocky outcrop.

He could see that the whole hillside, as Mary had warned, was now wildly sprouting with the flaming fire-worm minions. Just like the ones they had briefly battled in Mavis's Cavern. They were red hot and hissing and spitting venom everywhere, causing Mary to wriggle and writhe to keep out of their reach and so making it even more difficult for Roger to fly.

Soon the whole hillside was a teeming mass of fire-worm minions and all of course under the merciless mind control of Lord Morgrim.

Nimp soon discovered this himself too. Not being able to avoid them by flying.

"I seez vem, yoo two get on ver rocks. I vill try and draw vemz away from yooz," he cried.

Roger could see Lord Morgrim, still riding along the rock crack, now barely a hundred or so yards away from them. He gasped with dismay, realizing the Night Imps great danger.

"Look out, Nimp! You'll be trapped!" he cried out desperately. But there was nothing more he could do. The Night Imp was on his own.

The Night Imp was caught between the monstrous Lord Morgrim coming down upon him from above and the seething field of deadly fire-worm minions below.

CHAPTER 13:
OUROBOROS!

Nimp courageously jumped into the midst of the swarming fire-worm minions, distracting them from Roger and Mary, kicking and hitting out at them in a mad, whirling-dervish dance. And busily pelting them with his deadly 'Dark,' left and right. Roger well remembered how Mary had used very similar tactics when they'd both been attacked by the Cold Arbor Gang, only that yesterday morning, unbelievably not so many hours ago, he realized.

The fearsome fire-worm minions flung themselves at Nimp, in a united, maddened frenzy, trying to burn and bite him with their fiery tongues and sharp, acid-slimed teeth. Nimp was too quick for them though. He nimbly danced and darted away to one side of the rock ledge. And it worked. The minions were being drawn away from Roger and Mary and were now fully concentrating on him.

Roger glided onto the rocky shelf, and at last deposited Mary, with the Egg, safely on it.

Morgrim, however, was not being distracted. He was getting close and heading resolutely towards them. And a bit of puny rock wouldn't stop a mighty Creature of the Core like him; he'd just melt through it like the proverbial knife through butter!

For Roger, there was only one way to go – they'd have to jump over the edge of the rock shelf and literally have to fly for their lives. But what about Nimp? Nimp would be left alone, stranded and vulnerable. How could he save the Night Imp too?

Nimp saw that the children were trapped on the rock-ledge and that their only hope was to jump and to fly... and do so before Morgrim smashed them to bits! Roger could see this too, he had to just trust his wings and leap, taking Mary and the Egg quickly down the hillside and to the cover of the trees there. Roger could only carry one passenger and that had to be Mary. He knew that if he could then make it to the Quaggy with Mary it was very unlikely that Lord Morgrim would follow them there.

"But that Mad Morgrave is another matter entirely!" he thought worriedly.

Meanwhile, Lord Morgrim well knew that exposing himself to the Sky and the soon to be rising Sun and its deadly Daylight, alone and unprotected here on the Erf's surface, would be extremely foolhardy. Only a raving lunatic would dream of doing such a thing.

But Morgrim now let out a great bellow of victory. He could see his foe cowering on the rock shelf below with nowhere else to go.

He realized he could just smash into the rock-ledge and crush the Humdrums and smash the Dragon's Egg to bits too. But he really would have preferred a more enjoyable end to this hunting game of seek, trap and destroy. He'd particularly wanted to capture the Dragon's Egg if at all possible; with that in his possession he knew he could more easily placate and control his deranged brother, King Morgrave.

So, instead of just slamming into the rocky outcrop, where the children stood, he skidded to a halt several yards from it. The edges of the rock-shelf cracked and crumbled from the shockwave and Roger and Mary were sent flying, skidding and rolling towards the rock edge.

Mary, in fact, rolled right over the edge and barely hung there by the one hand, while also doing her best to keep the dragon's Egg safe under her coat with her other hand.

Roger seeing her plight quickly scrambled over to help her up.

As he was doing so the noble Nimp darted back and forth through the fiery minion hordes. The army of fire-minions was swarming about him and following in his wake, all now trying frantically to catch hold of him. There was now one great, seething mass of angry fire-worm minions between the immense bulk of Lord Morgrim and the two Erf children. And one of those was desperately clinging to the crumbling rock-ledge with the Dragon's Egg.

"Fly children! Fly, fly, fly!" Nimp cried out urgently to them.

Then, with an incredible leap for one of his diminutive size, he sailed over the fireworms and landed on the rock-shelf and stood there facing them, small but defiant; just him alone, between Morgrim and the two Egg-bearers.

He briefly turned and again loudly commanded, "FLY CHIL-DRENZ! FLY NOW!"

Roger pulled Mary up and onto her feet and gripped her tightly in his arms. The Dragon's Egg once again safely cushioned between their two battered and bleeding bodies.

"Brace yourself Mary, this could get a bit rough!" he told her wryly, preparing to jump.

Then Nimp hurled an enormous burst of his magical 'dark' at them. The cloud of darkness quickly enveloped them and at the same time knocked them off of the edge of the rock shelf. Thus, the decision to leap had been made for him. Roger didn't even have time to be stunned. He acted almost instinctively. Unfurling his bat-wings tightly holding onto Mary as he did so; he caught the updraft, blowing up the side of the volcano and turned his fall into a long, low glide, down toward the tree-line far below them.

As they again flew, Roger quickly looked behind him and saw the huge bulk of Morgrim, looming high over the rock-shelf and bearing down upon the small lone figure of the noble Night Imp, making his brave but futile, last stand.

Roger felt trapped and torn with guilt. He was in torment, impaled on the proverbial horns of a dilemma. How could he just leave the brave and loyal Night Imp to stand up against the might of Morgrim, all alone? But he knew, he had no choice, he just had to.

He saw they were barely halfway down the hillside but trees were starting to appear more and more frequently. And Roger's great bat wings were beating rhythmically at the air now as he dodged around the tree trunks. At last it looked like they could make it as they glided along, down toward the distant dim squiggle of the River Quaggy.

Yes, ahead, lay potential safety and survival; behind them, certain death and destruction. But also, a very good friend who had put his life on the line for them many times and was doing so again. "Could he just abandon Nimp now?" Roger thought tearfully. "Could he be the one that ran away from danger just for the safety of his own skin? The very thing he'd once accused the Night Imp of doing!"

Roger slowed and then haltingly hovered, and then with a large sigh, finally made his own courageous decision and so landed with a thump in a rock scattered clearing just below him. He lowered Mary onto her own two feet as he did so, and they stood there together, quietly, both well knowing what the other was thinking and feeling.

It really didn't need any fancy telepathic skills. They just knew.

"You're right, Roj," Mary said, quietly, "we can't just leave him there."

"But what can we do, Mary?" Roger asked her forlornly.

High above them, they could see the small, inky form of the Night Imp, darting about on the rocky ledge. He was hurling his many colorful curses and teasing taunts at Lord Morgrim, who was still looming above him and swaying threateningly from side to side, just like one of those Amerikan skyscrapers about to topple over, Roger thought to himself. And Nimp was mind-casting as well as yelling and cussing, so even at that distance, they could catch the full meaning of his very inventive invective.

Roger was just relieved though, that somehow, by some miracle, he was still alive!

"Who'z a yoozless squiggle-pigz thenz? Who'z juss a fat old fart-puffs then; a Morgy-Porgy; a wriggling old wigglez-poofs, eh? Youz iz, ain't yerz, Mor-grime? Nah. Yerz carn't catch meez, can yerz? Yer vile verminish vomitz; yer slimy sacks of slug-sicks!"

How Nimp was surviving was by being fast. And of course, by also hurling more of his Dark Bombs at the Fire-Worm Lord, as well as his abuse. Lord Morgrim was being buffeted about, much like a zeppelin being bombarded with a barrage of flak. He was avoiding the exploding dark bombs, the best he could though, as more than anything, they interfered with his acute mental powers, not to mention his vision, in the, to him, rarefied and horribly open, Erf-air.

As for the colorful insults, Morgrim was now steadily losing his temper with this impudent, meddling, miniscule mite of an Imp.

"We've just got to do something!" Roger muttered to himself. Then out loud he asked, "Are you getting all this, Mary? What the Pesky Pascal is that Imp up to, do you think?"

"Yes, I can hear everything. They're both very loud!" Mary replied. "But I think Nimp's trying to distract him, Roj. He's trying to buy us some time, so we can get away!"

But then all at once a scream of rage erupted in their heads, making them both grab at their temples, wincing with the sudden piercing pain!

They now heard a second but very familiar voice joining the mindcast!

"*They're getting away, Morgrim! Do you hear? They're getting away! You promised me – get them now, get them now!*" Morgrave bellowed, in a telepathic rage to his brother.

"*Stay calm, Morgrave. Stay calm and I'll get them, do not fear; they will never reach the Quaggy River; wings or not!*" Morgrim mind-cast back, trying to sound calm himself, but finding this increasingly difficult to do. The little gnat of a Night Imp was irritating him a lot.

"*But they're tricksy devils, I tell you. Who knows what that Worm Queen Sivam got up to with them? They might still be armed with Blue Fire for all we know!*" Morgrave raged.

Roger and Mary stood transfixed, uncertain of what they should now do. The wise thing, of course, was to flee for their lives, Roger realized. But somehow, he just couldn't do that. Not while he knew the valiant Night Imp was still alive. Maybe there was something they could do. Maybe one of his magic tokens would become active in some way; maybe he...

But then a particularly large and very noxious 'Dark Bomb' exploded violently right in Morgrim's face and the Fire-Worm Lord roared in livid anger; now having lost all patience with both his brother and the irritating Night Imp, who was still leaping about below him, jumping around and jeering insolently.

Roger felt in his own mind, Morgrim's patience suddenly snap, as he thundered angrily at his brother, all pretense of calm and reason momentarily deserting him.

"*Morgrave, just shut your manky mangy muzzle, will you?*" he raged and then he lunged forward, slamming his massive bulk down onto the rocky shelf where the Night Imp stood.

Roger watched in horror as the shelf was totally smashed to pieces. The last image he had of Nimp, was of his spindly, dark shape, standing valiantly at the edge of the ledge, hurling a final burst of 'Dark' that billowed and quickly obscured the whole scene.

Morgrim though, came bursting through the cloud, on the rampage. Intent now on getting to his prey and finishing them off once and for all, regardless of his getting the Egg or not. He'd had enough now. He was going to smash everything to smithereens! There would be no more running and hoping for escape for these puny Humdrums or that damned Dragon's Egg!

Roger and Mary quickly ran to a nearby thicket of stunted trees, for some slight protection, as a torrent of dust and debris cascaded down from the shattered rock-ledge above them.

But flimsy trees wouldn't be anywhere near enough protection against the irate Morgrim. Roger could see there was no way they could escape. They would never be able to out-run or out-fly the rampaging onslaught of the huge and enraged Lord Morgrim.

Not even his Bat Wings or Mary's enhanced strength could save them now.

And what had happened to their little guide, the courageous Nimp? Had he been killed; just cruelly flattened by the vile Fire-Worm Lord? Roger mentally searched for any telepathic connection with Nimp... but he couldn't sense a thing; not a glimmer of a fleeting thought.

The Night Imp's thoughts had suddenly ceased to exist!

Roger stood staring up the hill, totally aghast. The horror of their situation had become even worse! As Morgrim slammed and slithered his way over the crumbling remains of the ledge, a huge explosion erupted from the volcano's side, just below where Morgrim and the ledge had been. It was his mad brother, the current King of the Fire-Worm Lords, Morgrave.

He was on the rampage once again and had erupted from out the side of Hooter's Hill!

Morgrave was blind with blood-lust, let alone from the effects of Mavis's self-combustion having blinded his eyes. There was no way he could wait any longer, left wallowing deep within the volcano's Magma Chamber. He had to make certain of things himself, so he'd used one of the fumaroles, a fissure that brought gas and steam to the flanks of the volcano.

"Oh, by Humphrey Davy's Dumplings!" Roger swore. "Quick Mary, grab hold of me; we'll have a better chance in the air. Those two will smash us to bits if we stay here!"

Mary leapt up and grabbed Roger tightly around the waist, just as Roger flapped his mighty Bat-wings and wheeled up and away from the Erf-quake-scarred hillside.

On the hill above them, the two enraged Fire-Worm-Lords gave chase, but to each other – as well as to the two children. Morgrim hard on the tail of the mindlessly enraged Morgrave.

Mary looked around for any means of escape and saw none. And realized Roger was right. There was nothing left to be done but to fly and just pray for a miracle!

To the East, far beyond the Bad Wood, the dark horizon was starting to slowly lighten, at last heralding a new day, they might never actually see.

"Oh, Roger, I don't believe it!" she cried as they flew. "There's two of 'em after us now!"

Before he could answer though, they felt a huge whap of air, that blasted them right out of the sky, sending them tumbling down towards the stony ground. Roger was barely able to control their crash and Mary just barely managed to keep the Egg protected. Her enhanced strength helping her take the shock of the landing and the sonic-boom that suddenly hit them.

It was Mad King Morgrave who had sent his own deadly sonic-blast, booming down at them and knocking them out of the air like two flies under a giant's, invisible fly-swat.

"Ha-ha, yes! You, Humdrum scum! You won't get away from me, I've got you now!" Morgrave screamed in glee, laughing manically at them both. But then, he hesitated in his wild advance. In his excitement and blood-lust, he'd forgotten – he was blind and couldn't actually see them, especially up here on the deadly Erf's surface!

He could hear them and sense their heat though; and as Roger groaned, untangling himself from the prickly bush he'd landed on, Morgrave immediately lunged forward again, changing direction slightly, as he homed in on where Roger lay, sprawled helplessly on the ground.

"Shhh, be quiet!" Mary mind-cast to him. "He's blind but he can still hear us, Roj!"

But Morgrave could sense mind-casts too and quickly turned his attention towards Mary, sensing it was she who actually held the infernal Dragon's Egg.

Roger saw Morgrave was only a couple of hundred yards away from them and his brother Lord Morgrim not much further behind. He quickly scrambled to his feet and half ran and half flew to where Mary lay. He wasn't going to let that monster get to her, no matter what. He was, after all, her one and only Knight Irritant, he grimly thought, not feeling very much like a knight at all.

He flung himself forward and spread his bat wings; not to fly, there wasn't time for that, but to shield and protect her and the Dragon's Egg, from the Fire-Worm's murderous attack.

Roger felt a steely calm wash over him, as he awaited the arrival of the bludgeoning death blow. He scrunched up his eyes and just had time to mumble, "Goodbye, Mary" and then he thought to himself what a great adventure it had all been. Then he thought that at least he'd be able to go visit Gaia, the Erf Spirit, again. And Mary would probably want to do that too, so he'd probably be seeing her again soon. Then he thought... "Hold on, how come I'm still thinking all of this?"

He tentatively opened an eye and realized that he was still there, lying on top of Mary and that no bludgeoning death-blow had arrived after all!

Mary pushed him off of her, half crying and half joking, "Have you got a thing about jumping on top of girls then, Roj?"

"S-s-sorry Mary," he replied, helping her up and turning red as he did so, even knowing she was just ribbing him in her usual teasing way.

Then they both fell silent, gazing intently up the volcanic hill in disbelieving awe, up to where the two giant Core Worm Lords were now grimly embattled together! Morgrim had caught up with his insane brother and had grabbed him by the tail with his vice-like jaws and had brought him to a skidding halt.

The grunts and groans, cries and curses of the two battling brothers echoed in their heads. The ground around them splintered and fractured even more, as Morgrave writhed around, slamming his body back and forth, desperately trying to get free of Morgrim's steel-like grip.

"*What are you doing? Let me go you stinking, stupid slug-worm!*" Morgrave mind-cast, in mindless rage at his brother's outrageous attack. "*I will kill these Sky-vermin, I tell you; why are you stopping me?*" he screamed, worming and writhing about trying to break free.

"I am saving you – you idiot! I am trying to save us both!" hissed Morgrim. "Don't you understand? I can see, but you are blind – there, beyond the burning Wood – on the horizon. To the East, look, Morgrave. The Dawn is coming!"

Morgrave indeed had no idea about the thin band of pale light that now hovered hazily on the eastern horizon. He had been solely intent on his humdrum prey and nothing else.

But Roger, hearing this, looked for himself and could plainly see that the night was indeed nearly over. Soon that thin band would brighten and spread ever wider, and then splinter into the gold and ruby shards of the new morning's sunrise.

Roger saw that Morgrim was in fact very, very afraid of the Dawn. He suddenly realized that this must mean death for the Un-kind. He now understood; for a core creature to be on the surface at night, was one thing, but to be bathed in the Un-Erfly light of the newly risen Sun was quite another.

By means of his telepathy, Roger fully understood that no creature of the Core could survive such an ordeal. But even this wasn't enough to deter the Murderous Morgrave.

He was so close; it was only his treacherous brother, Morgrim, who was keeping him from what was rightfully his. His rightful Humdrum prey and royal revenge upon the Sivad's.

"Nothing will stop me, do you hear!" he roared, lunging and twisting with all his might.

Roger watched, half fascinated and half horrified as the leaner and lither King Morgrave managed to flip himself over Morgrim's bulky back. He then somehow grabbed hold of his brother's tail in his own jaws. Morgrim just barely managed to keep hold of the tail that he held tightly in his own jaws; and thus began, the extremely grotesque and gruesome sight of the two fearsome Fire-Worm-Lords, rolling down the hillside, locked together like one giant, Lizardish Hoola-Hoop. A ferocious wheel of fiery fury!

Roger could clearly see both their bodies were now steaming in the cool, pre-dawn air. The Erf's air itself was acting like a deadly acid on their hideous, armored hides. The oxygen-rich atmosphere was slowly eating into them and melting its way into their very innards.

"Morgrave, you must stop! We must leave now; we are not yet ready for this deadly surface air!" the bigger and wiser of the brothers, Lord Morgrim, mind-casted desperately, pleading for his mad twin to come to his senses. But Morgrave was deaf to such pleas, as well as blind of eye and rage. He had no intention whatsoever of stopping.

Roger watched, dazed and dumbfounded, as the Fire-Worms locked tail to teeth and rolled on towards him. They were about to be crushed yet again, but this time, by two Worm Lords!

"They're just like the mythical Worm Ouroboros," he mused to himself in his old detached and scientific way. "That's the ancient magical symbol of the serpent or dragon eating its own tail, continually devouring itself and being reborn from itself," he reminded himself.

Then he suddenly remembered Mary and decided he'd better quickly tell her just how very special he thought she was. Maybe there was just enough time for them to say goodbye too, but properly this time.

But, yet again, as if by some hidden hand of fate, it was Lord Morgrim who unwittingly came to their unexpected rescue. At the very last second, he managed to thrust his two thick, back legs firmly into the stony ground; and then suddenly letting go his grip on Morgrave's tail, he brought them both crashing down, slithering noisily to a halt, just a few yards from where Roger and Mary lay huddled, curled up together on the desolate hillside.

Roger gulped and glared grimly and glumly up at the huge Fire-Worm Lords above him. He knew that one or the other of them was about to either pound Mary and himself into dust, or just swallow them whole as nothing but irritating midges.

CHAPTER 14:
THE DANCE OF THE DRAGON SOULS.

T he sky was brightening quickly now. Roger saw the long, thin fingers of purple and gold, starting to stretch out, lighting up the greying sky. And he could see the two fallen Worm-Lords were feeling very uncomfortable indeed. Their normally invulnerable hides were now seething and steaming with streams of burning acid. They were like two long ranges of rugged volcanoes, about to erupt and spew out their fiery guts, all over the side of Hooter's Hill at any moment.

Roger realized, that although that would be a great and very fitting end to the two grisly monstrosities, it unfortunately would also be an end to him and Mary and the Egg as well.

But even though the maddened Morgrave was twisting and twitching about, in ever-increasing agony, he still stubbornly refused to turn away from his all-consuming course of revenge.

"Look, he's still trying to reach us, Mary, quick, get out of his way!" Roger yelled.

Morgrave was hauling himself inch by slow inch toward them. He was snorting and hissing. His eyes burned a sulfurous yellow like two, uncaring suns; aflame with hate and the insatiable need for his fearsome fangs to feed on Erfling flesh and for his claws to crack and crush the very last Egg of the Queen of the True Dragons.

"You will all die!" he hissed, now rearing up high over them both.

Roger saw the great bulk looming over him; as the long and eerily distorted shadows of both Morgrave and Morgrim flickered over the brightening flanks of the smoking hillside, and Roger could hear every curse and cry Morgrim made, as he desperately tried to reach his mad brother, and get him away from the Sun and the Sky that was slowly killing them both.

"If one Fire Worm dies, then both die, that is the Core Law, brother!" he hissed. "Stop this senseless suicide now! I command it!"

"That's very interesting!" thought Roger.

Morgrim was not willing to die or to relinquish his rightful turn of the Kingship of the Core. He had powerful plans, very secret and very important plans and he had to stop his brother from unwittingly destroying these. He somehow had to get them both away from this 'Heaven on Erf.'

Roger wasn't ready to die either. "Maybe my Magic Tokens will help us now," he thought as he grabbed Mary and they crawled over to the meager shelter of a few nearby rocks.

As he did so, he saw that the very sky above the Fire-Worms seemed to be on fire itself!

There were several great ripples and flares of reds and golds and then many other colors too. There were blues, greens, pinks, purples, magentas, mauves, oranges and yellows. In fact, there seemed to be more colors in the sky now than Roger had ever seen or heard of ever before.

It was the Dawn exploding into light and life and swiftly spreading over the fleeing firmament of the dying and defeated Night. The great and glorious Sun itself was balanced on the horizon, like a fiery eye of bright, shimmering gold, radiating yet again its morning message of hope and help and heat and health, to all life on Erf, of whatever kind.

Roger stood and tugged urgently at Mary, pointing up at the sky in amazement.

"By Oppenheimer's Unholy Homework! Mary, look!" he gasped. "Look, can you see them, can you see them up there? Oh, Mary, they're... they're... magnificent!"

The Morning Sky was now aflame with Dragons.

Mary stood next to Roger and gazed upwards; their eyes sparkling in the pearly dawn-light.

"Oh, Roger, yes... it's the Dawn. I can see them there Roj; there must be thousands of them! The dawn is the Dance of the Dragon Souls!"

The many fiery Dragon Souls were made from pure light and flame. They were burning so brightly, in their most splendid and radiant hues. And they were dancing; twisting and turning and climbing and cavorting; all whirling in a great fiery, flying circle.

They came in all the colors of the rainbow, in countless combinations! They shimmered and shone and swam and swooped in the morning sky, in glorious whirls of dancing dragon-flight.

Roger saw that the two Fire-Worm Lords now stood unmoving; both stunned and paralyzed and both totally transfixed before the dazzling display of the flaming dawn; the dawn that was, in fact, thousands of colorful and ghostly dragons, shimmering and shining in the resplendent light of the newly risen Sun. Wave after wave of the Dragon Dancers flew and whirled around the top of Hooter's Hill. The newly formed Hooter's Hill Volcano was crowned with a fiery cyclone of Dragon Soul Dancers.

"Look!" cried Mary again, now pointing excitedly to a particular and familiar dragon shape. "That's Mavis, Roger, look, it's our Mavis doing the Dance of the Dragon Souls, and, oh look, she's got both of her wings again!"

Roger just nodded dumbly, his eyes brimming with tears and mouth wide with amazement, drinking in the beautiful spectacle that was flashing and flaming all around him. He was still aware of the Fire-Worms of the Core, but he somehow wasn't worried. They were both helpless before the onslaught of dazzling light, color, and beauty above them. In fact, when Roger quickly peeked into Morgrave's mind, he found the King of the Core had now lost all powers of reason. He just foamed and fumed, mindlessly gibbering and quaking in fear where he stood.

But Roger could see that his brother, Lord Morgrim, was of sterner stuff, at least mentally. Looking into that dark and devious mind, he found that Morgrim, all too well, realized he and his brother had little chance of surviving, exposed to the Sky and the Dance of the Dragon Souls too. He knew that their only hope was to get away underground, and as fast as Fire-Wormly possible.

Roger heard him snarling and half pleading and half swearing at Morgrave. But his stubborn brother still blindly and resolutely refused to listen. He truly was beyond all reason.

"Those flimsy, filthy overgrown ghost-flies! I'll swat 'em out of the sky, I tell you. You bothersome, buzzing bilge-bees, you won't stop me. I'm getting that Egg, you hear me?"

Morgrave screamed on and on, completely oblivious to the deadly ravaging of his own flesh and bone. Morgrim realized any further pleading was utterly useless. Roger too felt the mental shock as Morgrim now fully understood that his brother, King of the Fire-Worms of the Core, was now nothing more than a mindless, babbling idiot and a raving zombie!

He had no choice. Just as Morgrave reared up once more, raising his bleeding and blistering hulk to crash down upon the Egg-bearers, Morgrim swung his huge, club-like tail, slamming it with all his strength and might into his brother's head and knocking him unconscious. He then again took hold of Morgrave's tail in his vice-like jaws, but this time, to drag him back to the nearest volcanic crack and so escape this hideous death of a thousand daylights.

Roger observed what Morgrim was doing but also saw that the Dragon Souls were not paying any attention to it. He then realized they weren't after blood and revenge; it was simply that such beauty and wisdom and goodness existed that it was naturally deadly to such dark beings as the Fire-Worm Lords. It was more than they could bear, just being in the presence of such things.

Roger watched spellbound, as Morgrim clawed and heaved his way rapidly up the hillside, dragging the mindless Morgrave with him.

Their hides boiling and blotching as they went; both of them slowly melting under the onslaught of joyous light and air. All the Dragon Soul Dancers swooped above them, regardless, just enjoying the freedoms and pleasures of their dance.

Morgrim soon reached the shattered area where the fumarole's mouth had been, the very one from which his now broken twin brother had leapt. He quickly and painfully slithered into the dark, fuming hole, dragging Morgrave in with him.

And so, at last, the two Fire-Worm Lords disappeared from Roger's view.

"They've gone!" Roger gasped with relief to Mary. "They've really gone!"

"Yes, thanks to Mavis and the Dance of the Dragon Souls!" she answered him, but then peering intently upwards, she worriedly asked, "But can you see any sign of Nimp at all?"

"No. Not from down here," Roger replied. "Come on, Mary, let's put our new Powers to use. Let's go back up to where that rock ledge was and look for him; it's the least we can do!"

Roger launched himself into the air and this time Mary pounded her way back up the hillside, her super-strong legs hammering up and down like two pistons. Roger had to dodge and dive his way around a few stands of stunted trees, so she just beat him to the large, steaming fissure, the very same volcanic fumarole, the two Fire-Worm Lords had made their escape by

Above him, Roger could see that the Dance of the Dragon Souls still spun around in the sky, but it was now visibly slowing, as the Dawn began to gently fade. The spectacular flight of the dancing Dragon Souls was slowly breaking up as the day grew older by the minute.

Roger landed next to Mary, at the lip of the smoking vent and looked up at where the shelf of rock had once been. It was the last place he'd seen Nimp alive. But there was no sign of anything alive there now. Mary stood and silently took his hand. Then together, they looked down into its eerie depths but there was nothing to see there but the smoke and the dark.

"We should have a look around just in case," Mary said, and proceeded to pick her way around the hole's edge, carefully stepping through the blackened rocks and the rubble and ash that were strewn all over the place.

But there was absolutely no sign of Nimp or any living thing whatsoever.

"I'll just scout around up above where the rock shelf used to be," Roger called back to her, taking off again. "I'll be able to cover more ground from the air."

He took the most direct route, flying right over the gaping hole and it was then that his magical Bat-wings suddenly faltered.

It felt like his heart had suddenly stopped as well. He could feel the Bat-wings were slowly withering and shrinking, as he fluttered over the fuming vent. He desperately flapped what he had left and desperately tried to make it to the other side. But then he stalled and started to spin out of control. He tried not to panic but he could see the dark, yawning gash of the vent right below his feet; like a hungry mouth, wide-open and ready to swallow him whole.

As he fell and spun, he flung out one clawing hand and managed to grab hold of a protruding rock at the vent's ragged edge. He hung, swinging and reaching desperately, to get a proper hold with both hands. He didn't have time to be scared, he just acted with a swift instinct that belied his swottish appearance. He clung on, holding on to the edge and yelled up to Mary for help.

But she was already on her way, having seen the whole thing. She came running as fast as she could; which wasn't that fast, seeing how the side of a shattered volcano isn't a very good place for running; but also, because her own super-strength powers were also rapidly fading away!

"Hold on, Roj!" she gasped, her breathing now becoming increasingly ragged.

She leaned over and hauled him up though, using every last scrap of the super-strength she had left. Roger lay face down, bruised and breathless himself. Seeing he was safe, she sat and looked down at the woods that stretched to the Quaggy river below them. She was completely exhausted, and then she began to quietly sob. Every shred of her super-strength had now left her. She felt like a dirty, battered rag-doll, thrown away and abandoned on some nasty rubbish-heap. Roger immediately turned to her and gave her an affectionate hug.

"D-d-don't cry, Mary; we'll make it... somehow. 'There is always a way to find a path that is worth the taking,'" he said softly, doing his best to mimic Mavis and looking into Mary's eyes with love and concern. "Remember, Mary, that's what our Queen Mavis says, right?"

Mary tried to smile at him and then wiped her eyes and nose.

"Oh, Roj! I know, but you don't understand!" she whispered to him, sniffing.

"I do, Mary, I do. I know how impossible it all looks and w-w-we've even lost our Nimp too and that upsets me a lot! I wasn't very g-g-good at learning from Dragons and Tree Kings at all you know. All this magical and spiritual stuff...it's hard to believe but... well, it just is, isn't it? So, we can't give up now, Mary, can we?"

"No, Roj, it's none of that. I know all we've got to lose for ourselves are just our own bodies; I get that bit, I really do! But we've got to save Regor, our Dragon's Egg; there's so much at stake, I know there is... but... but, that's not it either... look... look down there, Roj!"

Mary pointed over his shoulder and down the volcano's slope. Roger followed her finger and then saw and immediately understood what she meant. They had been delayed for far too long.

The forest fire had raged onwards... and had completely surrounded Hooter's Hill.

Their way back to the River Quaggy and home was now well and truly blocked!

Even Roger's thoroughly hard-won resolve and courage were now put to the test. He gazed down on the scene below in utter shock and could see nothing but devastation. Everywhere he looked was a blazing inferno!

Roger could see that the flames even now were licking along the banks of the River Quaggy, their one and only route out to safety and escape. And even worse, the forest fire was also making its way up the sides of the new volcano of Hooter's Hill.

Thick, acrid smoke was billowing all around from the conflagration of the burning Wood. Roger hoped the wind kept up its current course, mainly blowing the smoke away from them. But the safety of the River Quaggy was now definitely out of their reach; once again they were well and truly trapped!

"Oh, by Einsteins Eyebrows! Where do we go from here?" he raged quietly to himself.

Roger sat with Mary in his arms, dumbfounded and dazed. They had come so far and gone through so much together. Surely it couldn't end like this? He tried to keep in control of himself, he didn't want to upset Mary and give her any further reasons for despairing. "Surely though," he thought, "this must be a good time for one of the Forest Folk's Magic Tokens to help us out. It can't get any worse than this, surely it can't!"

He stood up and fumbled in his pocket and fingered the various objects, muttering to himself, "Come on then, one of you, say something for Frantic Freud's sake, just do something, OK?"

But it was to no avail. The magic tokens just lay dormant and dumb in his pocket; without a bleat, a bang or a burn from nary a one of them.

Roger stared glumly, and walked a little way, away from Mary. He didn't want her to see the tears that were now welling up in his eyes.

"Well, here we both are, all alone, exhausted and hurt," he grimly thought to himself. "Trapped on the side of an active volcano, that also happens to contain two murderous, magical Fire-Worm Lords, who hate us and want us dead. And we've lost our friend and guide, Nimp. And we've lost our magical powers too. Then, we've got rivers of hot lava flowing down toward us, not to mention a raging forest fire that has us completely surrounded and has cut us off from any hope of escape... and, and... no one knows we are here anyway... and, by Kepler's crazy Kippers, just what are we going to do now?"

"Oh, Roj, don't you start giving up! I'm sorry. We'll find a way somehow," Mary said, and then paused. "Hold on there, Roj, how come I can hear your thoughts again and use telepathy? We don't have any Dragons with us for that to work, now, do we?"

But there was a Dragon.

While they had been recovering by the volcano's vent, above them the Dance of the Dragon Souls had come to an end. The vast legions of dragon souls were fading away into the pure luminescence of the early morning light. But one Dragon Soul had remained. And it was Mavis, the one and only, Mother and Queen of the True Dragons.

Roger looked up, eyes wide, as he nudged Mary, now seeing and understanding who the Dragon was that had been enabling their telepathic skills again. He saw though that Mavis too was beginning to fade away. Her glorious colors of red and gold seemed to ripple and stream away from her, as she flew down towards them.

She then hovered over them, spreading her golden wings out wide. Then arching her neck, she blew a long and gentle breath over them both; warm and sweet and full of the unknown perfumes of the Spirit world of the Dragons. They were once again enveloped in the soothing, blue flame. The clouds of acrid smoke were all wafted away, and they heard her, singing in their heads once more, sending her calm and warming words of Dragon Wisdom.

"Remember children, there is always a way for a path to be found that is worth the taking."

Immediately their hearts were lifted, and their flickering spirits soared.

"Oh, Mavis, you're so wise and... and... so beautiful!" Mary cried out with joy.

"Thank you, my young Egg-bearer," Mavis laughed. *"Now empty your minds and allow the source of your true selves to shine forth; the simple but supreme Spirits that you both are!"*

Mavis slowly rose upwards and stretching her sinewy neck blew out from her flaring nostrils, two great gouts of pure, white flame, that twisted together high into the sky. The two entwined, radiant beams soared up like a rocket of bright, phosphorous fire, that then exploded high above them. Mavis then flew around them one final time, before leaving to rejoin her ghostly ancestors. But as she left, she sang, softly and sweetly, her final words of Dragon Wisdom.

"No more grieving, dear hearts, my trusted Egg-bearers; all things that pass will be once more; that which gives life and takes life never dies! That is Mother Nature's Great Law!"

With that she was gone, flowing away, as a faint flicker of red-gold flame, fading into the sky.

Roger stood in silence, stunned and dazed, upon the blasted flanks of Hooter's Hill Volcano. He felt that his heart would burst with joy. He had never ever felt so alive before, in fact, which he knew was totally mad really, for after all, by all reason and rationality, they were both still about to die! He could plainly see that there was no safe way down. They had been delayed for far too long. Hooter's Hill was now utterly and completely, surrounded by a sea of raging flame.

But somehow, by some unknown miracle, Roger didn't feel scared; he felt calm and at peace and just stood quietly with Mary standing next to him and once again taking her hand in his.

Together, they looked out over the horrific scene of fiery devastation, as the world of the so-called Bad Wood continued to burn below them. Roger remembered Mavis's oft-quoted words – and he now fully trusted in her ancient and mysterious Dragon Wisdom.

"There is always a way..." Roger whispered.

"Yes, always a way!" Mary answered softly.

Then, as if out of nowhere, Roger saw, high in the sky, a dazzling, white ball of light.

He blinked his eyes, to clear them from the vestiges of smoke, as well as from the sheer disbelief he felt. He could hardly dare to believe what he saw. He knew it couldn't be any of the Dragon Souls; they'd all gone. Nor could it be the Moon, as there wasn't any Moon that night.

Then he clearly heard it; there, sounding above the roar of the wind and the smoke and the crackling flames of the forest fire, he heard the unbelievable but insistent and unmistakable, whup-whup-whup sound, of a Helicopter!

They were saved!

CHAPTER 15:
PRINCE REGOR YRAM AWAKES!

Roger was momentarily dazzled and disoriented by the bright glare of the searchlight blazing down upon him, along with the thunderous noise of the helicopter's whirring rotor blades.

Repeated blasts of air slammed into him like a giant's sneeze and whipped around his ears, deafening him to all but the noise of the helicopter.

He peered through his fingers and could see the pilot skillfully controlling the chopper so that it hovered above them. An air rescue crew member then slowly winched his way down towards them. Roger saw that their would-be rescuer was standing on a cradle-like basket, as it jerked its way downwards. As he approached, he indicated for them to get ready to grab hold of it.

The red uniformed rescuer came twirling on down through the swirling smoke and sparks. Roger gestured for him to take Mary up first and the crewman duly obliged. Roger held Mary's hand for as long as he could as she ascended, then she was gone, spinning above him, briefly dangling like a tiny spider on a line of silk and then pulled up to the safety of the helicopter.

All at once he felt very, very alone. He felt exhausted and all mixed up inside. He was sad to see her disappearing away from him, but also happy and relieved to know that she was now safe.

With his heart in his mouth, he patiently waited the few heart-pounding minutes for the rescue line and the cradle to return, and then, at last, it was his turn. The same crewman helped to strap him firmly into the cradle seat and then his stomach lurched, and he felt himself rising upwards.

He looked down between his knees and saw the ground receding dizzyingly beneath him and swaying from side to side, as well as, starting to spin around. He felt sick, going green about the gills and his stomach starting to flitter and flutter even more. The rescue man steadied the cradle though and kept a firm grip on his shoulders. Soon, he too was alongside the chopper and for a short while, he could see the blasted side of Hooter's Hill stretched out before him.

It was a scene of dire devastation. Full of cracked and broken rocks, landslides of rubble and stones, and full of steaming fissures. Above, he could see the many rivers of molten lava still making their methodical way down the volcano's sides, spilling over from the smoking crater.

He keenly scanned every nook and cranny he could, looking high and low for any sign of the Night Imp. The whole hillside was becoming illuminated by the brightening light of the new day, as well as from the rosy glow of the forest fire. But there wasn't a thing to be seen. There was absolutely nothing left alive on that hillside whatsoever, Roger was certain.

Then he was up and found himself being hauled into the helicopter and the cabin door closed. The loud sound of the helicopter suddenly dropped to tolerable levels within the insulated cabin. He was lying next to Mary and she was smiling and safe. He smiled back at her and then winced, as he felt his stomach once again lurch and churn, but this time from the flight of the helicopter, as it turned and flew; thrumming its way over the Quaggy and the Good Wood, towards home.

"'Ello, you two. I'm Bill," said the rescue crewman in a cheery cockney accent. He helped them get more comfortable and gave them blankets and sips of water from a flask to ease their scalded throats. Roger could see that another rescue man was already inspecting Mary's injuries.

"We're takin' yoos two over ter the local hospital," Bill said gently. "Yer've both been right lucky, yer know. I presume yoo, young man, are Master Roger Briggs and this pretty young lady 'ere is Miss Mary Maddam, am I correct?"

"Yes! B-b-but how do you know that?" Roger asked, momentarily confused.

He was still feeling very weak and tired and found he now couldn't think very clearly at all.

"I'll juss take that as a 'yes' then," Bill smiled. "Yoo two 'ave been causin' a right ol' ruckus yer know! But first fings first, let's 'ave a look at yers an' we'll see what First Aid yer needs.

"My friend Mary's hurt more than me, can you help her, please?" Roger told him.

"Now, yoos just relax, son-shine," said Bill cheerily, "we'll gets 'er patched up awright, don't yer worrys yerself none. Me mate Frankie's been seein' to 'er needs already now ain't ee."

Mary looked over at Roger and gave him a bright smile and a quick thumb's up.

"I'll be all right, Roj," she croaked, "I'll be fine now I'm sure, don't worry," and then winced with pain as the other rescue-man, Frankie, felt around her leg, inspecting her swollen ankle.

"We'll get that in a splint right away, missy," he told her, a bit brusquely, but very efficiently wiping her ankle clean of the soot and dirt it was caked in. He began to bandage it up, telling her, "now this might hurt a bit, Miss, so try and be a brave girl if you can, understand?"

"Oh, she can definitely do that!" Roger piped up in her defense, smiling at him brightly.

"Ouch!" yelped Mary, as he applied the splints to her damaged leg.

"So, right, now!" Frankie said sternly. "Can either of you explain what you are doing out in the Bad Woods in the middle of the night and all by yourselves in a forest fire?" Looking Roger directly in the eye and making him feel very uncomfortable and somehow guilty.

Roger was in fact slowly turning beetroot-red with embarrassment and shame.

How could he explain just why they were out in the Bad Wood, and in the middle of a forest fire and a volcano eruption to boot? What on Erf could he possibly say? Roger decided that the best policy, in this case, was to say as little as possible and for now to play it dithering and dumb. So, summoning his courage yet again and forcing himself not to stutter and splutter too much, Roger put on his best worried look and apologetically explained.

"We were j-j-just out exploring, sir, and we sort of lost track of the time and got lost in those horrible woods and w-w-we're so, so sorry, aren't we, Mary? And we're really very sorry to have caused you so much trouble, sir, really we are."

"Awright, awright, calm dahn, young man." Bill now interjected, although feeling that Roger was being interrogated and intimidated far more than necessary. But Frankie just wrote down Roger's answers in his notebook and looking severely at them both, continued to question them in his sternest manner.

"Right, you two, now I'm Frank, the co-pilot here and I don't take kindly to being called out to rescue foolish kids who should know better. Don't you two know that the Bad Wood is a very dangerous place to go? You've been taught all about that at School surely; the wicked ways of the wilderness and all that. No one goes into the Bad Wood; even the Council Authorities don't! People tend to just disappear in there... and those that don't are never in their right minds again. Now give us your names and addresses and explain to me just what the Devil you two think you were doing out on your own in the Bad Wood? And no fibs now, you hear me!"

Roger realized Frank was much more abrupt and officious than Bill, who was a kindlier and more 'salt of the Erf' character. But Bill, seeing how agitated the children were had had enough of Frankie's bullying and came to their defense, saying, "Now don't yer be bovverin' them right now, Frankie, and we've already got their names an' addresses, as yer very well know, right? An' right now they juss needs ter rest, an' get over all the bloomin' shock an' what not; they've 'ad a close call an' there'll be plenty of time for askin' blinkin' questions later."

Frank just shrugged his shoulders and sullenly lumbered off back to the cockpit, muttering about bloody delinquents and the yoof of today being useless and a waste of time and space.

"Yer two just rest a bit now," Bill said gently. "Don't worry about ol' Frank there; just cop yerselves some kip; plenty of time for stories later," then winked at them and started to leave.

"Please, Mister," Roger asked quickly, before Bill had time to go, "can you tell us how you managed to find us? We thought no one knew where we were."

"No problem, sonshine, an' call me Bill," Bill answered. "Well, we got a report in from the local bobbies 'bout two kids oo'd gone missin' juss last night. Seems that Missy 'ere's Granny, an' speshly yor ol' Dad, a Councillor Briggs I believe, a right uppity fellow from wot I've 'eard if yer don't mind me sayin'. Well, 'e, in particular, was causin' quite a fuss an' bovver over yoos kids at the local bobby shop last night. Was freatenin' all kinds of fings, 'im bein' a member of the bloomin' Under Lundun Council an' all!"

"Really!" thought Roger to himself, amazed. "My Dad causing a fuss and worrying about me, well I never!" He could hardly believe it. But he just said to Bill, "Oh, I see, th-th-thank you."

"Yes," said Bill, "an' wot wiv that blinkin' rocket flare goin' up like that this mornin'... well, yer've 'ad some right proper luck there, ain't ya, lit up the 'ole sky an' pointed you out to us as good as a finger in the eye! Probably wouldn't 'ave found yers at all wivout that bloomin' flare! Real Good Luck that was, having a distress flare handy like that!"

"Yes, what g-g-good luck!" Roger stammered, somewhat sheepishly. He felt even more guilty at having to pretend to be so dithering and dumb. He could see that Bill, at least, was a nice and friendly sort of chap. But he wasn't about to tell him or anyone else, that they never actually had a flare. They'd had a Dragon Spirit – not a flare. But who on Erf was going to believe that!

"And thank the old God yer were on the side of that there volcano where we could find yer," he continued, "I just 'ate ter fink wot could 'ave 'appened uvverwise, son, I really do!"

Then he left them to their own thoughts, and they sat silently and sleepily together, in the warmth of the whirring helicopter. Roger sat looking out of the small window, just watching the last of the fading sunrise on one side and the blazing conflagration of the Bad Wood on the other.

The dawn had been a glorious sight, reflecting the terrible rage of the forest fire, with its streaks of gold and crimson, as if the sky and forest had been battling each other with paintbrushes!

Huddled next to Mary, he sat quietly lost in his thoughts as the helicopter whirred onward. But just then Mary felt something moving; there was a slight shudder against her stomach. The precious Dragon's Egg was still wrapped up under her coat, and she had been holding it tightly to her tummy and now it was moving about, with tiny, repeated thumps. Their baby dragon was definitely alive and well!

"The baby Dragon's OK, Roj, I just felt it move," Mary whispered.

"You sound just like a pregnant woman," he quietly laughed.

"Well, I'm not a pregnant anything, thank you very much! But we do have a baby Dragon that we're going to have to make sure gets born, don't we?" she replied somewhat huffily.

"Yes, sorry," he apologized. "Well, Mavis told us that in order to hatch her Dragon's Egg, we'd have to keep it wet and cool, and then when it's ready, take it to the 'Dragon's Nest' where it can properly hatch," Roger answered, with his 'I'm thinking serious thoughts' expression.

"Yes, and all we have to do is get it to this 'Dragon-Nest' place somehow, wherever that is!" Mary huffed. "An' all Mavis told us was that we'd be told where, when the time was right!"

"I know," Roger mused, "doesn't give us a lot to go on, does it?"

The Dragon's egg remained quiet for a while, but a few minutes later Mary felt more bumps beating against her tummy, as the dragon foetus moved about, as if it were getting restless.

"We'll just have to get it to whatever water we can at first though," she sighed. "Oh, Roger, what are we going to do? How are we going to get the Egg away from here safely?"

Roger took her hand and said, as confidently as he could, "Don't worry, Mary, Mavis said it won't hatch for a while and we'll know when it's ready. We've got two problems to solve. One: We need to keep it safe and out of unwanted hands right now, and Two: We'll then need to keep it somewhere safe and wet and out of the way until we can get it to the Dragon Nest to hatch."

But Roger knew that the Dragon's Egg had to be gotten somewhere wet and safe very quickly in order to avoid embarrassing and dangerous questions about it. They'd never hear the end of it if they were found to be harboring an unhatched Dragon's Egg!

He thought about it, but after a while just told her. "We'll come up with something, Mary!" And then returned to his thoughts. Just where could they hide and keep the Egg safe?

He then brightened and exclaimed. "By Pasteur's Pants! As for number two, I've got a plan!"

He'd thought of the perfect sort of a place for hiding and keeping a large rock-like Egg wet, but first, he realized, there was the small matter of getting it there undetected by the authorities.

Roger knew that as soon as anyone saw the Egg, they'd see that it was something strange and very Un-Erfly and start asking difficult questions and demanding even more difficult answers.

And there weren't any good answers they could give, not any that would be believed anyway.

"Somehow we've got to disguise it, right now, before we land," Roger mused to himself.

"Yes," Mary sighed. "Definitely before we land, or someone's bound to find it when we do!"

"But how and as what?" he thought back to her, still concentrating on the problem at hand.

"Well, it has to be as something that won't bother anybody, you know, something ordinary, that won't cause any fuss," came the clear reply from Mary, directly into his head!

Roger sat bolt upright, stunned and amazed.

"Wha-a-a-t are you doing in my head Mary!" he yelled telepathically, alarmed at suddenly realizing that he was hearing Mary's thoughts again and she was hearing his. *"Mavis has gone, Mary! We shouldn't be hearing each other's thoughts anymore. We can't mind-cast. We can only do that when there's a Dragon around to help us, remember?"*

"Yes, exactly," smiled Mary, thinking cheerfully and clearly, in his head. *"We really would need a Dragon to help us do that, wouldn't we, and that's exactly what we've got, Roger!"*

Then into their heads came some child-like but clear and dragonish thoughts of introduction.

"Hewwo, Wodjer. Hewwo, Merwee. I'm Reegor, an' I'm verwee pweased to meet yous!"

Roger yelped out loud in surprise and Mary stifled her gasps of spluttering laughter.

"You two young'uns all right over there?" called out Bill; having heard Roger's sudden cry.

"Yes, fine, thanks," answered Roger. "Must have dozed off. Had a bit of a nightmare, sorry."

"No problem, son," answered Bill. "Yer just rest, it'll be over and done wiv soon enough."

The two children settled back down and to anyone watching they would have just been two very exhausted kids, wrapped up in blankets and seemingly fast asleep. In fact, they were now very, very wide awake and were into a deep and extremely 'thoughtful' conversation. However, there were no longer just two people in this conversation.

The baby Dragon, as named by his Royal Mother, Prince 'Regor Yram,' (though currently, still un-hatched), had at last woken up! He was barely more than a lizard-like tadpole, curled and wrapped up inside his leathery dragon egg casing; but he was now fully, wide awake!

The subject under discussion was that of the immediate need to disguise the Dragon's Egg in some way so that it wouldn't attract any person of authority's attention. Both Roger and Mary were feeling quite stumped on that one.

"I could pretend to be a bit dotty," Mary thought to them, "and that the Egg is a sort of comfort blanket that my mum gave me; then I could start crying if they try and take it away!"

"Not bad," thought Roger, "but way too risky."

"Don't wowwy, me thinks mees can help," baby Regor thought brightly to them both.

"Oh, please do!" they thought at once, replying together.

"OK. It's awwl done, you can takes a wook now," the unborn Dragon thought back to them, confidently.

Mary quietly and carefully unwrapped the Dragon's egg from beneath her coat. And there it was, lying there as plain as a gray day in May: a perfectly ordinary, round, lump of rock. It was a dull grey and smooth, like any normal stone and about the size of a rugby ball.

"What have you got there?" called out Frank, who had suddenly come up unheard behind them, to tell them they were about to land so they had to lie down and buckle up.

"Don't wowwy!" whispered Regor Yram in their heads. *"Shows him, it'll be awwight."*

"Oh, we've just got a nice rock as a present for Roger's mum and dad, for their fish pond, that's all," piped up Mary pleasantly. "Look, do you think they'll like it?" she asked, showing him the rock, lying innocently in her lap.

"Barmy kids!" muttered Frank. "Looks a bit boring, if you ask me," then gruffly told her, "anyway, time to belt up now, we're about to land." And with that he left them to it, not having the slightest interest in their silly present of a boring old rock, meant for some smelly fish pond!

"*Told yoos,*" laughed Regor, in their heads. "*Mees juss a chip off the old block, mees is!*"

Soon the Helicopter was landing, and Roger could see below him orderlies with stretchers and trolleys ready to take them into the Eltingham Hospital.

"Well, we're here and now we've got to get through all the barriers of the Humdrum Human World and keep Regor safe and take him to wherever he needs to hatch," Mary sighed.

"Yes, that worries me too." Roger telepathed back. "Just how are we going to get Regor out of this Hospital to a safe place... and just where in the Blazin' Bunsen Burners are we supposed to take him to, to get successfully hatched, anyhow?"

Mary couldn't answer that. But Roger thought it best to change the subject and cheer her up.

"I don't know how we did it, but, we 've made it Mary. Where safely back in Under Lundun!" He grinned. "And if we can make it through the Bad Wood then I reckon we'll make it here too!"

CHAPTER 16:
A BREAKFAST OF CHAMPIONS!

With that, the Helicopter landed with a shuddering jolt. Frank sat with the Pilot, and as usual, just ignored them, but Bill stood and waved a fond farewell to them as they were taken away.

Mary just had time to call back, "Thanks for your help, Bill, you've been very kind."

Roger quickly called out to him too. "Yes, thank you, Bill," and then they were gone.

The two hospital orderlies took them straight from the Helicopter into the Hospital and wheeled them along the long, green corridors to the waiting room outside the Casualty Wards. There, they were told they would be assessed by a Doctor and that their Parents would be seeing them before they were put into their respective Wards.

They lay on the trollies next to each other and continued their telepathic conversation while awaiting the arrival of their next of kin and the Doctor who was due to assess them.

"There's something else worrying me, Mary," Roger telepathed to her after a few moments, as they lay taking in the bustling sounds and antiseptic smells of the Hospital environment.

"What's that, Roj? You don't have to worry about me now you know. I've been knocked around a bit, but I'll pull through."

Roger lay on his back and bit his lip.

"Yes, I know you will, Mary, but, well... it's just that so much has happened to us. I don't know how I'll ever be the same... and, well... the truth is, Mary... I'm scared!"

"That don't matter, Roj, we're both scared, but you're just about the bravest person I've ever met, an' that's tellin' yer straight." Mary smiled over at him.

"Thanks, Mary. I appreciate that. But it's not just the monsters and the dangers we've faced... it's... well, it's something else." He groaned mentally.

Mary realized that Roger was doing his best to confide in her something deeply troubling him. "Go on Roj, you can tell me. We're friends forever, right? You can tell me anything!"

"I think I'm becoming a Dragon!" he blurted out to her mentally.

Mary gasped but kept her reaction under control.

"What do you mean, Roj? I can tell you fer nuthin' you're still a boy an' you don't have no wings or scales or claws and whatnot. You're definitely not a Dragon!"

"No, not like that, Mary," Roger replied. "I mean on the inside. There's something going on inside me and it scares me. I felt it really, strongly, back up on those rocks on Hooters Hill. You know when I called up the Red Flame and incinerated all those slug worm things."

"Yeah, you were brilliant up there! Real hot stuff I'd say!" Mary laughed, trying to keep things light and cheerful between them.

"No, it was horrible, Mary, I could have easily got carried away. I don't know what could've happened. I don't think I was ready for that kind of power. I've just got used to doing the Blue Flame shield thing. But the Red Flame. That's something else. That's a terrible force!"

Mary just mentally nodded. She'd wondered herself as to just what was happening to Roger. He seemed far more adept at Magic than she was and there seemed to be a unique and special bond growing between him and Regor.

"Anyway, Mary, I think there's a lot more we need to learn about Magic and Dragons, not to mention the Great Forest of Lundun and the Under Erf itself!"

Regor now butted in, piping up in their heads with his bright but babyish way of talking.

"*Yesh Wodjer, you ish right. But don't worries, when I'm borns I'll teaches yous, OK?*"

"Thanks, Regor!" Roger laughed. "I s'pose my learning about Magic from a newborn baby Dragon will be an interesting and new experience for me, to say the least!"

"*Yesh it will!*" Regor continued, unphased. "*I'm already membering things about ush!*"

"What do you mean, about us?" Roger asked, intrigued.

"*I means about us Dwagonsh, of course!*" Regor replied. "*I knows that wees have thwee Dwagon magics to learns abouts. But I'm still memberings about them as I grow. I thinks I'll learn much mores when I'm born!*"

But before Roger, or Mary, could respond, the waiting room door burst open and Roger and Mary were at last reunited with their anxiously waiting nearest and dearest. Namely, Roger's wailing mum and frowning dad and Mary's beaming Granny Maddam.

Roger's parents had been making a lot of fuss with the police and the nurses and doctors too. Mrs. Briggs had spent most of the time sobbing in a corner of the Police Station's reception room; burbling things like, "Oh, where did we go wrong, Brian, just where did we go wrong, eh? we brought him up to be a well-behaved boy, didn't we? Oh, Brian, where did we go wrong?" And then snorting her motherly woes into a sodden handkerchief.

"Well, you've got some explaining to do, haven't you, my boy?" said Mister Briggs, sternly.

"Oh Roger, Roger! The shame of it!" cried out Mrs. Briggs, still sobbing and dabbing at her puffy face. "What on Erf have you been up to, Roger, and how could you? You've been brought up to know better! Oh, really, what will the neighbors think?" she wailed in trumpeting anguish.

Roger looked up at them, and then over at Mary, who lay quietly, still clutching the rock-like Dragon's Egg under her coat. Mary gave him a quick smile and a thumb's up and then he heard Regor telepathically blowing a little raspberry in his head, obviously aimed at his parents.

Roger smiled and suddenly felt quite calm and composed. He felt that he'd not actually done anything wrong at all. He'd just tried his very best to save his new friend as well as help save the Dragon's Egg and all that meant to the world too. He lifted his face to his mother's and said to her quite slowly and firmly and without a trace of his old stammer.

"It's all right, mother, we've been exploring and having adventures, that's all. And you know what, I really don't care what the neighbors think about it at all. But I'm very happy to be alive!"

"That's right, Roger," Mary giggled telepathically, "you tell 'em, you're now Sir Roger of the good old Bad Wood and a brave Knight and a very good egg too, as far as I'm concerned!"

"*Yay, meez too!*" echoed Regor in his head. "*Meez a good Egg too, meez is!*"

Roger and Mary snorted out loud with laughter at this, but Mr. and Mrs. Briggs had no idea as to what they found so funny. They just stared blankly, nonplussed at their strangely changed son, as if looking down upon some previously unknown alien creature.

Mr. Briggs, at last, got over the shock. "Leave the boy for now, Gladys, he's obviously not in his right mind. I will ensure that the very best Brain Surgeons and Psychonomists are called for, of course, I promise!"

With that, he turned stiffly back to his son and said, "We will discuss this matter another time, Roger. For now, please see that you disassociate yourself from this, this common girl and her kin." He flicked his eyes towards Grannie Maddam, who had been silently waiting in the background. "You well know that I am standing for election as Prime Councillor this year, Roger. So, I, therefore, expect you to conduct yourself accordingly. We can't have members of the Psychonomy alarmed by the willfully aberrant behavior of the son of a candidate for such high office. Is that understood, my boy?"

Roger inwardly froze and bit his lip. He lay quietly on the trolley and refused to say or do anything to acknowledge his Father's imperial commands.

Mr. Briggs saw that his son was obstinately refusing to say anything, so he snapped at him, "They're keeping you here overnight for observation, Roger, but I'll be collecting you tomorrow and from here on, you can consider yourself grounded!"

"Blistering Boyle! That's going to make it even more awkward to get Regor away safely!" Roger thought to himself.

But now Grannie Maddam stepped forward. She'd had just about enough of this pompous, posing and posturing politician.

"Yer not a Guvverment Minister yet are yer, Mr. Briggs. Yer a Father, so why don't you's act like one, eh? Yer boy here, he's been through quite an ordeal as I sees it an' now ain't the proper time fer any blamin' an' shamin', right?"

Mr. Briggs turned towards Grannie Maddam, momentarily stunned. But then quickly pulled himself together and blew a snort of disgust through his mustached lips.

"Do you mind, Madam! This is a private family matter and is of no concern of yours, at all! I would ask you to take your ragamuffin Ward away to wherever she belongs and leave me to deal with my..."

At this point, Mr. Briggs was cut off in full flow.

"Yer talkin' rot and rabbits!" Grannie Maddam hissed.

She drew herself up to her full five foot four of height and jabbed a finger at Mr. Briggs chest.

"I will not be talked to in that..." began Mr. Briggs once again but to no avail. Grannie Madam thrust her chin up and her eyes blazed, glowing with a deep purple glow, drilling into Mr. Briggs'.

"You won't talk at all if yers not careful Mister Braggs!" she threatened menacingly.

"It's Briggs, and I'll have you arrest... erk, I'll have you arrk... I mean, I'll av yoz arrekked, I meanz... squirk... stop thish... squiggle, squirgle... immediamental, I meanz... wosh happeninins to mees?"

"Looks like you've lost your lovely polly-tickle voice, don't it?" Grannie Maddam chortled. "Oh, dearie me. Well, best gives yer moan-phone a rest then, eh!" she finished airily.

Then turning her attention towards Mary, she chortled. "Hello there, me Love. You've been in the Woods now, ain't yer? Yer silly Pickle!"

Mr. Briggs abruptly turned about and left the Ward, dragging the damp and distraught Mrs. Briggs along with him, stammering and squawking as he went.

"Well, good riddance to bad rubbish, I says!" Grannie Maddam muttered under her breath.

Then she surged forwards, arms outstretched to take Mary in her arms for a very big cuddle. "Oh Mary, my love, I'm so happy to see you," she cried out in joy, and hurled herself onto her beaming grand-daughter, giving her a huge hug and very sloppy, wet kisses on her cheeks.

"Ouch!" Mary yelped and laughed. "Do mind my ribs, Gran, I'm still a bit sore you know!" But she hugged her Gran back, as best she could, with a wide grin on her dirty, elfin face.

Roger felt a bit jealous at seeing this open display of familial love and affection. It made him feel sort of nervous and fidgety. It wasn't something he was used to at all.

Old Grannie Maddam was a kind and clever old lady though. She easily recognized the signs of the loneliness and despair that lay at the heart of Roger's family problems.

She bent down towards him, saying, "And it's a pleasin' pleasure meetin' you too, my young man. I can see that you's been a good friend to my wilful little Mary the Minx 'ere and I'll bets you's any-thing she's been a handful for yers too, ain't she?" Then she winked at him, crinkling her sparkling, blue eyes. "So, here's a kiss an' a hug fer you's too, Master Roger!"

Roger found himself briefly smothered in the bosomy hug and bristly, wet kiss on the cheek that she adamantly blessed him with.

But Roger had never been kissed by anyone before. Not even a peck on the cheek. His mother considered it 'unhygienic' and his Father just thought it decidedly 'unmanly!' Roger though, now felt a warm feeling flowing through his whole body. He liked it. But he still couldn't stop himself from turning beetroot red with embarrassment.

But just then, he felt a sudden sharp pain in his leg. "Oh, what is it this time?" he thought, impatiently. "We're safe in hospital now, there can't be any need for magic tokens, surely?"

But there was something. Something wrapped in his hanky, that had come alive. Just like the golden acorn and the vampire tooth before, and that something was now burning into his leg.

This time though, he quickly found that it wasn't actually one of the magical gifts from the Tree King's Courtiers - but was some of the stuff they were all wrapped up in; it was in fact... all the wood-bark shavings that had comprised the bulk of the Owl Pellet!

He'd groped inside his pocket and carefully and as discreetly as he could, had pulled out the hanky and spilled the white bark shavings into his open palm and then carefully handed them to Mary. Having suddenly realized what they were.

"I think these are meant for you, Mary," he said quietly, handing them to her.

Mary beamed as she took hold of the precious and the much sought after, White Willow Bark.

"Oh, Roger. That's wonderful. Thank you. I mean, you, I, well... we, got this for you, Gran," she said, turning to her dear Gran and pouring the strands of healing bark into her wrinkled hand.

Old Grannie Maddam at first didn't know what to say. Tears welled up in her eyes, and then instead of saying anything, they both 'talked' to each other by throwing their arms around one another again, in another emotional embrace. Roger looked bashfully on, once again turning red and not really knowing where to look or what to do with himself.

Gran winked at him. "Yer better get used to hugs an kisses, if yer goin' ter go around saving damsels in distress," she told him.

Then turning back to Mary, she added, "And thank you fer the kind thought, Mary. I'm so happy yer back with me. I 'ave been worried yer know. But as I said, nows not the time for bad words and blame. I loves yer, dear, an' yer can tell me all about it once yer gets settled in 'ere."

"Oh, Gran, I do love you. And I'll tell you all about it, I will... but, I'm not sure you're going to believe half of it!"

"That's alright dear. Anyways. I been thinking. It's no good me goin' on at you misbehavin' when I've been doin' plenty o' that meself! Truth is, I've been lettin' meself go a bit o' recent. An' I'm goin' to do me best to change me ways. I'm gonna smoke less an' drink less an' get meself better – long as you promises to do the same, OK, dear?"

"What, smoke an' drink less? I don't think I can do that Gran!" Mary laughed.

"No, silly. Get better is what I mean. I want you out of here as fast as you can make it, right?"

"It's alright Gran, I was just joking with you. I know what you meant – and yes, let's both get better... and I hope the White Willow Bark helps!"

"It will I'm sure, dear. Now, there's another thing you should know... well a few things really, but well, first off there's been some mean gossip goin' round about us o' recent. Stuff about us being vagabonds an' Gypsies an' such. And that bully of a boy at your school, Josh the Cosh they call him, he's been mouthin' off to the Police about how you went crazy-mad in the Good Wood and attacked him and then went running off across the Quaggy an' draggin' Master Roger 'ere off with you just to drown 'im."

"What!" Roger cried out. "It wasn't like at all... we were..."

"Now, now, Roger, don't fuss. I knows more about what's true an' what's not than most have had fried eggs fer breakfast," Grannie interrupted him. "Anyways, dear, just so yer knows what we're up against. Things might get a wee bit rough an' ready round our way for a wee while," she finished.

And just then their happy reunion was interrupted. Two young Nurses and the Doctor, a smart looking, white-coated Indesean chap arrived, and the children were now officially turned over to them for their medical assessments and care.

"Hello, Doc," Gran piped up, "so what's yer prog-noses, how long do yer need 'em in for?"

"Good morning to you, Ma'am. Children. I am Doctor Maggam," he replied, with a little bow. Then speaking directly to Grannie Maddam, in a kindly, professional manner, he answered her. "Well now, I expect your young Mary here has got several days in Hospital ahead of her at least. But Master Roger though should be all right for a clean bill of health by tomorrow, so he'll be able to get off home to his—" (Here he gave a sarcastic cough – news of Roger's troublesome and rude Parents had traveled very quickly!) "—ahem, to his loved ones, all the sooner."

Doctor Maggam then bent over the children in turn and said in a confidential and kindly tone, "Now I bet you young adventurers are both really hungry, eh? Well, you're in luck; you're just in time for a good breakfast. The Nurses will take you to your Wards, one for the girls and one for the boys. They'll get you cleaned up and then see that you get two or three eggs down you right away for a nourishing and hearty breakfast. How does that sound then?"

"Eggs!" screeched Mary and Roger together, looking at each other in horror and trying desperately to stop themselves cracking up with laughter. "Oh no!" they cried, "no, no, no, just the one Egg we already have - is more than enough, thank you very much!"

And then they both burst out laughing, uncontrollably and with tears of joy as well as relief, streaming down their soot-stained cheeks.

"*I don't sees wot'sh so funny!*" Regor telepathed to them rather huffily. "*There's nuffin' wong with Eggsh is there? An Eggsh as good a place to start froms as anywheres!*"

THE END

EPILOGUE

Lord Morgrim's journey back to the Core was a very troubled one. But it wasn't his own wounds or even his wounded pride, so much as his grave concern for his brother; the blind and crippled Morgrave that troubled him. This deep concern though was not a kind-hearted and brotherly one; oh no, Morgrim's concern was for how his stupid, ignoramus of a brutish twin had come so close to totally ruining all of his carefully laid plans.

He had wrestled and pulled the half-dead bulk of his brother's wrecked and wreaking carcass down the long winding throat of the fumarole they had escaped into and had finally sunk into the heart of the volcano's seething main magma chamber. There they had some time to rest awhile and to prepare themselves for their descent to the Core.

Morgrim well knew that help was needed in order to achieve this though, especially as their journey had to be done as secretively as possible. It was absolutely vital that no one knew of the true condition of his brother. It was as certain as fire means power that the rest of the Fire Worms of the Core would in no way tolerate being ruled by a mindless, gibbering idiot. They would turn on them both, probably to the utter destruction of the enfeebled Morgrave and then at the very least banishment and degradation for himself. This could not be allowed!

There were only ten Fire-Worm Lords left alive and two of them were Morgrim himself and the current king, his twin Morgrave; so, he only really had the eight left to worry about. But he knew each pair of Fire-Worm Lord twins, had many hundreds of thousands of minions at their service and each Fire-Worm Lord was also very skilled in the arts of mind reading and mind control and manipulation.

But Morgrim was the most cunning and resourceful of all the Fire-Worm Lords. For many years he had been placing together the deadly pieces of his dastardly master plan.

Throughout the time of the rule of his brother, he had been secretly forwarding his plans and he had done so due in no short measure to his own unsurpassed mental powers. No one, not even his own brother, was aware of his secret laboratories where he kept his pet Humdrum scientists.

Using a primitive telecaster cap, Morgrim now sent a low-frequency Mind-cast on a very narrow beam directly to the particular help he required; specifically, that of two greedy and evil Psychonomists, the Inglishe Doctor Sydney D Mudfinger and equally venal but even more deranged Skiltish Doctor Rab Idego.

"I must return to the Core undetected with my brother. You must rapidly equip me with a vanguard of armored Black Dragons to ensure that we arrive safely and without arousing one iota of suspicion from any quarter. Do you understand?"

Morgrim waited but a few seconds until the weak, tinny and reverberating sound of Dr. Mudfinger came crackling into his mind. Mudfinger, being a Humdrum, was not very adept himself at such things as telepathy and other such mental powers; this was ironic really; him being considered such an expert on the mind. But what he was actually an expert on was the perversion, domination, and destruction of minds, and it was these particular dark skills that Morgrim now most required.

"Dr, Mudfinger zzzzt, here your, zzzzt Lordship. Please, let me zzzzt adjust the frequency of zzzzt this headset zzzzt!"

"Listen to me, Mudfinger, send me whatever Black Dragons you have prepared as ready, immediately! Just make sure they are able to perform as per specification. All our plans may rely on this. I must bring my brother back to our Core Fortress as quickly as possible but with no one knowing of his condition. Your own futures and very great rewards rely on this too. You understand? Now, how many can you send me?"

"Just let me zzzzt confer with my colleague zzzzt Dr. Idego a moment, Lordship."

Morgrim could barely hear the brief babbling exchange of concern occurring between the two Psychonomists as they exchanged hurried expletives and information.

They finally arrived at a conclusion and the burr-like tones of the Skiltish Dr. Rab Idego now rattled in Morgrim's mind, clearer this time as they'd fine-tuned the frequency.

"Och! Yur Lairdship, 'Tis I the indomitable Doctor Idego here. We cannee send yurs that many o' the wee black beasties at all ter be frank, not that wees can really relies on yur sees!"

"Just how many, Doctor? Answer me. I trust you know how important this is. How many?"

"Well, Aye, I understand yers o' course, Lairdship. Doctor Mudfinger and I, well, we, och, we believe wees can safely send ye thirteen o' the inky critters; will that do ye now?"

"Harrumph," grunted Morgrim, "it will have to do! Dispatch them all to my location now, immediately!" With that, he mind-cast them his exact location in the magma chamber under Hooter's Hill and then terminated the mental connection.

Morgrim knew that the Black Dragons would be with him in but a few hours. They had to travel through the secret corridors of the Erf's mantle from deep under Skiltland in the north, but the Black Dragons had been bred and trained to perform super dragonish feats of both mind and muscle. They could evaporate rock and minds faster than a flamethrower could cut through freshly laid snow! They could also create a web of silence, a mental void of absolute noiselessness, one where no other mind could penetrate and in fact would not even have any inkling that there was something to penetrate. It was this particular skill, which would greatly augment his own skills, that Lord Morgrim now required.

"I must ensure Morgrave continues his allotted rule while I go forward with my plans," he thought to himself. "I must arrange things, so the other Core Worm Lords are not stirred and concerned in any way. My plans are too important for they will put paid to the pesky True Dragons once and for all, not to mention all that ghastly green life on the Over Erf!

As he daydreamed, a broad crocodile smile of satisfaction stretched across his curling lips that he sensuously licked with his flickering, forked tongue, as he lay wallowing in the searing-hot sludge of the volcano's magma pool.

"Oh yesss." he hissed, "all Hell will be let loose and I, Lord Morgrim, the one and only - True King of the Under Erf, will rule all!"

Look out for the next adventure in the Dragon's Erf saga, Dragon's Flight, coming soon from S.R. Langley:

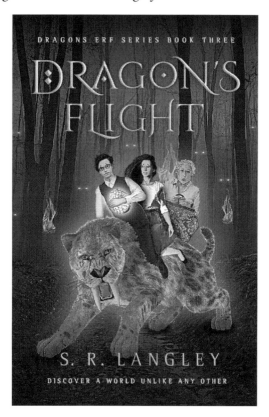

Dragon's Flight
DRAGON'S ERF SERIES BOOK 3

THE WORLD OF PLANET ERF HAS BECOME FULL OF SE-CRET ENEMIES AND HIDDEN CONSPIRACIES – AND ONLY ROGER BRIGGS AND MARY MADDAM HOLD THE KEY TO THEIR EVER BEING UNMASKED – THE UNBORN DRAGON PRINCE – REGOR, THE LAST SURVIVING HEIR OF THE DRAGON DYNASTY!

But can Roger overcome all the obstacles in his way? Can he save the Dragon's Egg and escape the evil clutches of the Psychonomy... and all the malevolent forces of the Core?

And it doesn't help that Regor, the last Dragon Prince, is already proving to be more than a handful for Roger – and he's not even been hatched yet!

And to make matters worse Roger now discovers something so utterly shocking he has no choice but to act. And act fast!

But he has no choice, he must save his best friend Mary Maddam and take flight with her and his precocious Dragon's Egg before the dreaded Psychonomy incarcerates them all.

And if the Dragon's Egg falls into the wrong hands – then all is lost – not only for Roger, Mary and Regor – but for the very Erf itself!

Follow Roger and Mary's incredible adventures as they delve deeper than ever into the unknown mysteries and magical wonders of the Great Forest of Lundun.

There they will find friends and foes in equal measure – some new – some old.

Roger knows, the Dragon's Egg must be kept safe – but to do so he and his friends must brave untold dangers and make it across the fire-blasted Black Heath to the River Tymes and the sanctuary of the Green Witch.

Will they make it?

CHAPTER 1: 'HOMES' ARE WHERE THE HATE IS.

Mary Maddam was bored but also worried. It had been well over a week now that she'd been kept in this "horrible horse-spit-an'-tell" as she called it; although, in truth, it really wasn't that horrible at all. It was a clean and orderly hospital, and the nurses in fact were all quite nice.

The Matron though, was something else. Matron McCracken was of the 'old school;' a real spare the rod and spoil the child sort of tyrant; all strict discipline and total adherence to hospital rules; rules that were always to be immediately obeyed and without any question.

But it wasn't the tyrannical Matron or the tedium of the daily routine of the place that was really getting to her. It was the absence of her best friend Roger. As expected, he'd been discharged from the hospital the day after they'd both arrived, and she hadn't seen hide or hair of him since.

He had managed to visit her just the once though, the day he'd left, just before being picked up by his angry Father, Councilor Briggs. And in those brief minutes Mary had managed to give Roger the Dragon's Egg; the extremely precious Egg of the, as-yet un-hatched, Dragon Prince, Regor Yram. The Egg they'd just rescued from the Dragon's Cavern and very nearly died for.

Roger had quickly concealed the rock-like Egg within his overnight hospital bag. His bully of a Father had then come storming into the ward, loudly complaining to the agitated nurses.

"I'm not having my son mix with this sort of riff-raff" he'd yelled, "that ragamuffin, that 'Mad' Maddam girl, is a bad influence on my boy. How dare you let her anywhere near him!"

The Ward Sister had hurried over and tried to calm him down the best she could, but by then he was in full swing and there was just no stopping him.

"Get the Matron here at once!" He'd angrily demanded of the Sister. "You know who I am, don't you? I demand to see the Matron at once, do you hear?" The cowed Sister had then obediently run off to find the Matron.

However, despite his Father's grandstanding histrionics and while he'd been distracted with such, Roger had quietly kissed Mary on the cheek, saying not to worry and had quickly told her: "It's alright Mary, I'll look after Regor and I'll come back and visit you as soon as I can."

Mary of course had done her best to ignore the very rude and personal attack on her from Mr. Briggs. Before their wild adventures, into the Bad Wood and the Dragon's Cave and everything that followed, she would have been a lot more sensitive about it. But she was now made of much sterner stuff; As indeed was the budding young scientist, Roger.

Just as Roger was leaving the ward, with Regor now safely hidden in his bag, she'd clearly heard the unborn baby Dragon telepathically calling out to her.

"Don't yous wowwy Marewee, it'll be awwight, pwomise! I'll look after Wodjer an' we'll all be backs toogevva soons, okays?"

But with baby Regor's talking ability still not being fully developed it meant that she ha to take extra-special care to work out exactly what he was saying.

Mary was still getting used to their new telepathic ability, kicking in whenever they were near the baby dragon. But this was just one of the many differences their recent adventures had made.

Then all mayhem erupted; Matron McCracken had arrived!

"What is the meaning of this!" She'd bellowed. "This Maddam girl has caused a great deal of trouble and has led this poor boy astray. He is not to be further infected by her low morals and despicable behavior. Do I maker myself clear?" Then of course the Ward Sister and the Nurses had been given another severe telling off, and all in front of the patients too.

Mary then saw Mr. Briggs speaking to Matron McCracken as he left, dragging Roger with him.

Mary couldn't quite hear all they'd said though, just a few words here and there. Matron had said something about "taking the necessary steps" and Mr. Briggs had gruffly replied, "well, see that you do Matron, the Special Under Lundun Council is relying on you!"

She briefly wondered what the S.U.L.C. was, "never heard of that one before!" she thought. But then her Gran had turned up. Mary could see her looking for her through the ward door windows.

Then she chuckled to herself, "that's a right laugh, me poor ol' Gran's lookin' across the Ward, tryin' to find her Ward!"

But then it wasn't funny anymore. Mary saw that two big orderlies had marched up, along with Matron McCracken, who now seemed to be forcefully steering her Gran away from the ward.

For a moment Mary couldn't see what was happening at all, but then a few seconds later she heard a loud scream and her Gran then reappeared at the door and stepped briskly into the ward.

She brushed herself down and made her way towards Mary's bed, holding a bag of grapes and waving at her with a big, beaming smile on her round, red and friendly face.

"Sorry about that dear," she said "seems there was some sort of a mix up as to who I was and whether I was actually allowed to visit.

No worries though; it's all sorted now. That 'orrible McCrackers woman seems to have taken ill and those big fellas have wandered off, oh well!"

***

BIOGRAPHY:

S R Langley is a… Writer and Poet.

Born last Century in the year of the Rabbit, he was raised in the Warrens of South Lundun, but after 18 years in the leafy suburbs, set out to seek his fame and fortune on the High Seas.

After some years circumnavigating Planet Erf, getting dizzy and then bored, he eventually returned home to his beloved Inglande where he finally caught a girl, settled down and after several years had gone by, discovered he had a family of five children, two cats and a dog!

He now lives in the vibrant Capital of the North West – and yes – he does of course support the greatest Football Club ever!

***

And don't forget…
Check out his Author Website at: https://www.srlangleywriter.com
And you can follow him on Facebook at: @SRLangley.Writer
Or on Instagram at: SoRoLangley or Twitter at: @LangleyWriter
Or you can email him at info@srlangley.com
And he will always be very pleased to hear from you and will do his very best to reply!*
(* Doesn't apply to Anti-Social Twits though!)

Subscribe to my newsletter to hear when the next book is coming out!
https://www.srlangleywriter.com/subscribe-contact

Printed in Great Britain
by Amazon